In Love and War

Lady De Lancey   Sir William De Lancey

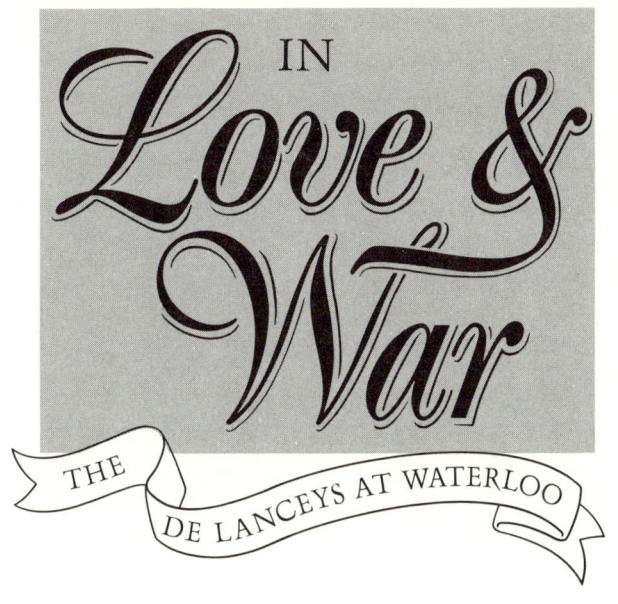

JAMES B. LAMB

Macmillan of Canada
A Division of Canada Publishing Corporation
Toronto, Ontario, Canada

Copyright © 1988 by James B. Lamb

All rights reserved. The use of any part of this publication reproduced, transmitted in any form or by any means, electronic, mechanical, photocopying, recording, or otherwise, or stored in a retrieval system, without the prior consent of the publisher is an infringement of the copyright law.

Canadian Cataloguing in Publication Data

Lamb, James B., 1919–
   In love and war

ISBN 0-7715-9208-6

1. De Lancey, William Howe, Sir, 1781?–1815—Fiction. 2. De Lancey, Magdalene, Lady, d. 1822—Fiction. 3. Waterloo, Battle of, 1815—Fiction. I. Title.

PS8523.A415I5 1989   C813'.54   C88-095370-5
PR9199.3.L352I5 1989

Jacket design by Helen Mah
Maps by Bo Kim Louie
Printed in Canada

Macmillan of Canada
A Division of Canada Publishing Corporation
Toronto, Ontario, Canada

I was born on a battlefield—what are the lives of a million men to me?

Napoleon Bonaparte

Contents

Foreword	ix
De Lancey	1
The Rascal Army	15
Magdalene!	33
After the Ball	49
The Babes in the Wood	61
The King of Spain	77
Waterloo	87
A Sea of Horsemen	105
Victory	123
Odyssey	135
Honeymoon Cottage	153
Aftermath	175

Foreword

In New York today, the De Lancey name has been given to an East Side street, and the family home is preserved as the city's oldest building. In Canada, a De Lancey is celebrated as the founder of New Brunswick, and in Great Britain another De Lancey is remembered as Wellington's brilliant young Quartermaster General, the man who selected the field of Waterloo for history's most famous battle.

But it is in the world of romance that the De Lanceys shine brightest, as a pair of lovers tossed on the tide of great events, and whose tragic idyll still moves the heart and uplifts the spirit.

This is a true story, of real people and actual events.

1
De Lancey

THE BAY OF CORUNNA was a tossing waste of wind-driven water, a gray wilderness flecked with hundreds of sails and loud with the shouts of hard-pressed seamen and the flapping of canvas. There were ships everywhere, more than three hundred of them, transports and warships alike, as British naval might struggled to extricate a British army from yet another tight corner. Time was precious; already the wind, now blowing half a gale from the southwest, was showing signs of backing. In a matter of moments it might settle in from the north, making this whole roadstead a lee shore and a fatal trap for the heavily laden transports clawing off under a press of sail to find sea room on this dangerous, reef-strewn coast.

It was mid-January, 1809, and here off the northwest extremity of Spain the winter wind bit cruelly. The little knot of officers on the quarterdeck of HMS *Endymion*, one of the Royal Navy frigates that would escort this enormous convoy once it had embarked its human cargo, were muffled to the ears in heavy boatcloaks as they watched the last stages of what had become almost a routine operation for British seamen: the landing and embarkation of an army. This one was now well advanced; from the *Endymion*, telescopes were trained on the jetties of the little town tucked under the lee of the projecting headland, where the transports alongside were already embarking the rearguard. The long files of dark green strung out along the waterfront could only be the rifle regiments of the famous Light Brigade, the new arm created to fight in a new way with a new weapon and vigorously trained by Sir John Moore. Yesterday, as the spearhead of the British army, they had won a notable victory in the mountainous heights above the harbor, but there was no elation in the somber files now shuffling aboard their transports. This morning, in the silent hours just before dawn, they had buried their commander, the man who had taught, trained, and led them with such patience all these years. His shoulder torn away by a cannonball, Moore had died in agony surrounded by his riflemen at the very moment of victory. They had buried him, wrapped in his cloak, on the grassy counterscarp of the citadel above the town, "and left him alone with his glory."

Then, in sullen silence, they had filed down into the streets of the town, their boots worn through, their uniforms in tatters after the most terrible march ever endured by a British army. For weeks they had been the rearguard that kept the French at a distance while the troops struggled through the wintry mountains of Spain. Now, bearded, wild-eyed, and haggard, they bore so fearsome an aspect that the townspeople crossed themselves at the sight of them, and shrank into doorways as the weary columns clanked past.

Aboard *Endymion* and the crowded troopships in the roadstead, however, spirits were high. Not only was the embarkation proceeding well and the wind favorable, but yesterday's victory had brought an elation that not even the loss of a brilliant young commander-in-chief could dampen. After weeks of retreating from an enemy they despised, it had been a rare tonic for the weary British regiments to come to grips with the French again, and send them reeling back down the road they had come. No matter that Moore's death, at the climax of the short, fierce battle, had robbed them of an even greater victory; for the exultant red-coated infantry of the line regiments it was enough to see their blue-coated French counterparts scurrying in disarray down the steep slopes to escape the murderous musketry of Baird's and Hope's divisions.

Why had the French allowed themselves to be caught this way, by an enemy on the very point of departure? The naval officers aboard *Endymion* were convinced it was due to a miscalculation by Marshal Soult, the French commander. Eager for glory, like all Napoleon's generals, he had overreached himself. After a perfunctory reconnaissance, his scouts informed him that the British had embarked all but a scanty rearguard. He had advanced rapidly along two mountain roads to outflank the British lines in the mountains above the town, hoping to take easy prisoners from the rearguard and set up his artillery on the heights to harass the shipping in the harbor below. Instead, he had himself been outflanked by defense positions still strongly held; the heads of his columns had been blown away by the British volleys and both roads enfiladed by plunging fire. His attack was brought to a standstill; it became a retreat, then a rout. As his desperate troops fought to escape back down the narrow mountain passes, Soult watched helplessly while French dead and dying encumbered the densely packed roadways. Only the death of Moore, the British commander-in-chief, and the resultant hesitation in following up his victory, allowed Soult to escape the ignominy of a complete disaster at the hands of an army bent on departure. Napoleon himself would hear of this shortly, and Soult would have some difficult explanations to make, *Endymion*'s officers agreed, and shook their heads in glee as they relished the French marshal's discomfiture.

Inshore, the work of embarkation was rapidly reaching the final stages. In addition to the troops boarding transports alongside in the harbor, British soldiers were standing in ragged lines along the full sweep of the foreshore that extended from the town on its hillside to the west, to the mouth of the Rio Mero in the east. The boats of the fleet were hard at work ferrying troops from the beach to the transports anchored offshore. Husky naval seamen were pulling anxious soldiers aboard, two at a time, and packing them down on the floorboards of the navy's big cutters, launches, and gigs, before pulling away from the sand, crowded with redcoats.

These were all infantrymen, now; the cavalry had been embarked the day before, and there had been some rare scenes for the watching seamen to enjoy. There had been room for only a thousand horses on the crowded cavalry transports, and the word had gone out for the remainder to be destroyed on the beach so that they would not fall into the hands of the French cavalry, which was desperately short of horses. Each trooper was ordered to shoot his own mount, and indeed those under the direct gaze of their officers did so, using the short cavalry carbine to fire the fatal shot.

But the British soldiers, even these men calloused by months of fighting and hardened to human suffering by campaigning in a country where hardship and cruelty were endemic, were notoriously sentimental about animals. Ordered to destroy their horses, with whom they had shared so many vicissitudes, many of them instead simply fired their carbines into the sand, smacked their horses on the backside, and allowed them to gallop off along the beach. The shore of the bay had been a maelstrom of plunging and rearing horses, a confusion of shots and shouts, and the curses of furious officers. Hundreds of horses had been given to the enemy, but to the watchers on *Endymion* it was all a huge joke, another instance of the army's curious way of doing things.

But now, something else was capturing their interest.

The officer of the watch, a lanky Scots lieutenant named Basil Hall, was focusing his telescope on a small boat running out from the harbor, which now drew the attention of the other observers on the frigate's quarterdeck. There could be no doubt about it: the boat was making its way directly toward them, inviting speculation as to what its purpose might be. Painful experience had taught *Endymion*'s officers that boats from shore with urgent messages meant trouble, more often than not, and they viewed the oncoming craft with misgivings.

She was a little coastal fisherman, scarcely larger than a rowboat, but heavily built with the high, bluff bows typical of vessels in this part of Spain, where rough Atlantic weather was the norm. Her buff-colored lugsail bellied out as she ran down before the brisk offshore breeze, and *Endymion*'s telescopes showed three passengers in her stern sheets, in addition to the seaman at the tiller and his mate crouched forward by the mast. Red coats and gold braid—they could only be British army officers. The high leather shakos showed two of them to be from a line regiment; the third seemed to be bareheaded. "Probably lost his headgear over the side in this wind," Hall muttered, as he inspected the newcomers; he had a poor opinion of soldiers in small boats. He turned and passed the word for a couple of seamen in the waist to stand by to take a line if the boat came alongside. But the occupants of the boat, it appeared, had no intention of coming aboard. While still some distance away, the little vessel rounded up into the wind with a great flapping of canvas and the bareheaded officer in her stern shouted up to the quarterdeck high above him: "Which ship has embarked the 45th Foot, please?"

Good God, thought Hall, the fellow must be mad; it could be any one of the three hundred transports that filled the whole horizon. Putting his speaking-trumpet to his lips, he explained the situation as best he could and invited the trio, whom he could now see to be soaked through and shivering with cold, to come aboard.

"No! No!" responded the bareheaded spokesman. "We must find our regiment's transport if it takes all day," and he gestured to the boatman to get under way again.

Hall's exasperation now got the better of him; these fools could never find one particular ship in this multitude now under full sail; they would be left behind on the hostile coast. With a peremptory bellow, he ordered the boat alongside, and grinning seamen quickly handed the three crestfallen soldiers up the side.

Once safely aboard, the three made their way aft to where Hall awaited them, and introduced themselves. All were officers of the 45th Foot, but one of them—the hatless one—was serving as a junior member of Moore's staff. They had been separated from their regiment in yesterday's fighting, and had hired a boat in an attempt to catch up with the transport on which their unit had embarked early this morning.

As patiently as he could manage, Hall explained to them the impossibility of a small boat overtaking a square-rigged ship in the strong wind that was blowing, let alone the difficulty of finding one particular ship from among the hundreds in the bay.

"Come along with us," he invited. "We'll take you home, and make you more comfortable than you could be on any crowded troop transport."

"But that's just the point!" exclaimed the young staff officer, who had introduced himself as William De Lancey. "We want to share the same conditions our fellows are enduring. How can we face them if they think we've gone looking for a cushy berth home in a navy ship?"

Yet for all his protesting the young soldier could see that Hall's argument was all too true: there was simply no possibility of finding his regiment's transport among the press of shipping that filled the horizon in every direction.

Bowing to the inevitable, the three accepted the invitation of their naval hosts, and were led below to inspect their new accommodation. Each was allotted a berth in a tiny canvas cabin, more like a closet, shared with a ship's officer, and a seat at the long table running the length of the wardroom. For men who had been campaigning for weeks in the bitter Spanish mountains, this was luxury indeed, and when *Endymion* weighed anchor a few hours later and stood out of Corunna Bay in the wake of the last crowded transport, her three passengers were happy to be aboard.

Despite contrary winds and the difficulties of keeping so large and diverse a collection of ships in some sort of formation, the long run northward to Ushant and then eastward to the Lizard proved uneventful. Since Trafalgar four years before, French naval operations had been minimal; it was only the occasional privateer that attempted to interfere with British shipping now, snapping up any unescorted merchantman they could catch in the chops of the Channel.

For the first few days, the three army officers in the frigate's wardroom were celebrities of a sort. Their faces and characters, their backgrounds, and, above all, their experiences during the long war were a welcome change in a closed community in which everyone knew nearly everything about everyone else. The two young subalterns, Palmer and Harding, had been with their regiment in the Peninsula for only a short time, having arrived with a draft of reinforcements, and their experiences were soon described. De Lancey, though, was a major, and had been with Moore from the beginning of the arduous Spanish campaign, and his stories, particularly of the army's fighting retreat over the mountains, were avidly followed by *Endymion*'s officers.

No one was more interested than Basil Hall. Between the tall naval officer and the dedicated young soldier a fast friendship grew; both had similar views on the conduct of the war and on a wide range of other subjects, although they were of widely dissimilar backgrounds and temperaments. Hall was an even-tempered Scot, whose chief interests lay within the service, and an able, energetic naval officer. De Lancey, on the other hand, was a young fire-eater, intelligent and ambitious, who governed himself by the highest standards but whose zeal was offset by a quick understanding and great personal charm. To the bemused Scottish sailor, this dynamic bundle of energy and talent was a fascinating fellow indeed, and during his watches below, Hall learned a good deal about his friend's exotic background.

To begin with he was an American, born in New York to a notable Huguenot family which had produced several distinguished soldiers, jurists, and administrators, and whose name was associated with the development of New York City and the founding of North American thoroughbred-horse racing. William had gone to England to complete his education and had entered the army there. His father had purchased him a commission as a cornet in the 16th Light Dragoons while he was still a youth, as was then the custom for young men of "family" wishing to follow a military career.

In 1796, at the age of fifteen, he had transferred to the 17th Light Dragoons, a smart regiment commanded by his uncle Oliver, but had found the cavalry's social pretensions at variance with his youthful notions of soldiering and was glad of a posting to an infantry unit, the 45th Foot, a line regiment with a solid fighting reputation. He had settled in, rising to the rank of captain and then major.

When the regiment returned home in 1802 from service in the West Indies, he was selected to serve as a staff officer, and was posted as deputy assistant quartermaster general, with a wide range of administrative and operational duties. After garrison duty at York and then in Ireland, he had been appointed to the staff of Sir John Moore, Britain's most promising young field officer, with the army then being dispatched to fight the French in Spain. It had not been an easy campaign. "It wasn't the French who bothered us," De Lancey explained. "We learned how to handle them; it was the Spaniards who gave us so much trouble."

The Spanish had proved the most difficult of allies; indecisive, tardy, quick to take offense at any fancied slight, they had driven Moore half mad at times with exasperation. And ultimately, of course, they had caved in under French pressure, their capitulation leaving Moore's little army stranded in hostile territory, cut off from supplies of any kind, and with no option but to make a fighting retreat through the mountains of northern Spain to the Biscay shore and the succor of the British Royal Navy.

That retreat, which had reduced a fine British army to a rabble of starving, wild-eyed savages, had left its mark on the impressionable De Lancey, yet to Hall's amused surprise the emaciated young officer seemed to burn with the desire to come to grips again with the French.

"We know now how to beat them!" De Lancey declared, pounding his clenched fist on the quarterdeck rail. "Wellesley worked out the tactics that gave us the upper hand when we beat the French three times in a single day at Vimeiro." With quick jabs of his finger sketching imaginary lines on the teak rail, he explained to Hall just how it had been done.

"Up until now Boney's had it all his own way, he and his marshals, beating second-rate generals fighting the old-fashioned way. But now at last in Sir Arthur Wellesley he's met his match."

The French revolutionary troops that Bonaparte had inherited had great élan but little formal training, De Lancey went on. They lacked the discipline to maneuver on the field of battle in the long, orderly lines of old-fashioned conventional armies. Accordingly, Bonaparte formed his infantry into columns rather than ranks, solid blocks of men in very close order, thirty men across by forty-two men deep, and he sent them into action behind a cloud of sharpshooters and light field guns.

A typical Bonaparte battle consisted of a tremendous cannonade by the massed artillery, which was the most formidable arm of the French service, and which decimated the long ranks of old-fashioned European armies. Through the smoke of the cannonade the shaken ranks would perceive a wave of French soldiery advancing in dense columns behind scores of field guns and running snipers, who paused momentarily behind any available cover to send balls and bullets whistling into the English ranks at ever-closer range. As they drew closer, the columns began to trot, their massed drums beating the *pas de charge*, their leveled bayonets gleaming, and the tall bearskins of the leading grenadiers seeming to make their front ranks eight feet high. It was a fearsome sight, and few armies were steady enough to stand up to it for long, particularly when squadrons of the heavy French cavalry dragoons and cuirassiers simultaneously assaulted their flanks.

But young Wellesley, who with Moore had been the only capable field commander to fight the French, had seen the fatal flaw in the French tactics.

"In the French column, only the front thirty men can fire their muskets; the rest simply provide mass," De Lancey pointed out. "British infantrymen are the first troops Bonaparte has encountered steady enough to stand up to his columns in long, unbroken lines. The British line, two ranks deep with the front rank kneeling, means every musket can be brought to bear, and at Vimeiro they simply blew away the head of the French columns. The thirty French muskets leading each column were no match for the concentrated British firepower."

Furthermore, Wellesley and Moore had found the answer to the usual pre-battle French cannonade. By positioning their armies for any set-place action on rising ground, and having their men lie down, in ranks, on the reverse slope of the hill, they were safe from cannon fire. "When the French sent in their columns, they found an army rising up to meet them at the top of the hill whose long lines were unbroken, and whose disciplined volleys, delivered at the word of command at very short range, were utterly devastating," young De Lancey concluded, his eyes alight with enthusiasm. "Properly commanded, British infantry will beat the French every time!"

But good British commanders, De Lancey added sadly, were rare indeed; Moore and Wellesley were the only exceptions to a long list of bunglers and incompetents sent out to command British forces in the Iberian peninsula. De Lancey had worshiped Moore, whose military capacity had been complemented by an appealing personality and great strength of character. His death, the young staff officer maintained, was a national catastrophe.

"Wellesley is our only hope now," he confided to his naval friend. "The troops know it as well as the officers, but the War Office back home keeps sending us nincompoops who just aren't up to their job."

There were few aspects of the war in Spain that had not been thoroughly discussed by young De Lancey and Hall by the time the convoy reached the Channel, and when *Endymion* at last shepherded her charges up the Solent and dropped her anchor in the crowded berths off Spithead, her tall lieutenant wrung the hand of his departing army guest with a good deal of warmth.

"I shall miss our conversational afternoons," he said regretfully as he saw De Lancey over the side into the waiting boat. "You must come and visit us at Dunglass when you've got a few days' leave. Even if I'm not there, Father would enjoy meeting you, and you can be sure of a warm welcome."

It was a casual invitation, but it was to affect the whole course of De Lancey's life.

On arrival in London, De Lancey was pleased to find orders awaiting him: he was to join the staff of Sir Arthur Wellesley and proceed with him to Portugal, where the British were proposing to land a considerable army to cooperate with Portuguese forces in resisting the French invaders. This was welcome news indeed; he greatly admired Sir Arthur and was eager to return to the Iberian peninsula, and to the active campaigning where a young officer could expect action and, with luck, promotion. Equally welcome was the permission to take three weeks' leave. He was a free man until the expedition should begin to gather in time for sailing early in April.

But his good spirits were as nothing compared with the exhilaration of the friend who pounded at the door of his London lodgings one night just after De Lancey had retired to bed. It was his naval companion from the *Endymion*, but it was no longer Lieutenant Basil Hall, Royal Navy, who threw off his rain-soaked hat and wrung his hand with fervor.

"Shake hands with the newest captain in the Royal Navy!" his friend shouted. "I've just been posted captain."

For a professional naval officer, captaincy was the all-important rank, the plateau which all strove to achieve. It meant security—a captain drew half-pay even if not employed—the responsibility of command, the opportunity of building a reputation and, perhaps, making a fortune in prize money.

It was a great achievement, and De Lancey duly congratulated his friend before telling him his own good news.

"And you're on leave now? Why, that's splendid!" Hall

exclaimed, clapping his nightshirted friend's shoulder. "You must come up to Scotland with me and share our good fortune with the family."

It was, accordingly, a jubilant pair of young men who arrived at the Hall family seat on the eastern outskirts of Edinburgh. The cold spring drizzle and wisps of fog drifting in from the Firth of Forth did nothing to dampen their spirits.

Dunglass Hall was a remarkable establishment. Built on the site of an old Carmelite college, founded in 1453 and long ago reduced to ruin, the Hall stood on rolling ground with a fine view of the sea, handy to Dunbar to the east and only a mile from the village of Cockburnspath to the south. The fashionable architect Richard Crichton had designed a house in the classical fashion, in deference to the antiquarian tastes of Sir James, with pediments and pilasters and architraves to delight his patron's eye. As reminders of past history, there was a charming little gazebo with Doric pillars and a domed roof like a miniature temple on a nearby hillock together with an antique sundial. Nearby, the Collegiate Church of St. Mary, a low stone building with a squat tower not far from the new Hall, had once served the ancient monastic college as a chapel. A little brook, the Dunglass Dean, ran through the grounds, spanned by a bridge with a crenellated parapet.

All in all, it was a charming place, reflecting the interests and enthusiasms of its owner, and De Lancey was delighted with it.

He was equally pleased with its owner. Sir James Hall, fourth baronet Douglas, proved to be a kindly gentleman of a scientific turn of mind, who passed most of his time in his study and workroom. A widower, he left the management of his house and much of the entertainment of guests to his unmarried second daughter, Magdalene, Basil's favorite sister.

Although at first she was a little shy of the handsome stranger her brother had brought home with him, she listened entranced to their chatter about places and people and happenings in a glamorous world remote from the sheltered life she was accustomed to in this backwater. Her quiet manner masked a lively wit and an ardent nature, and once the first formalities were past, the three young people fell into an easy relationship, forever laughing and talking.

For De Lancey, the days passed far too quickly; the weather had cleared shortly after their arrival, and the trio had made the most of the glorious spring weather with a round of picnics, long walks, and longer rides through the wooded countryside and along the coastline. All too soon the time came for him to take his leave, and the long post back to London. His stay at this friendly house had been the happiest time of his life, and he shook the hand of his, by now, best friend with genuine emotion. But it was even harder to take his leave of Magdalene, whose fresh beauty and sparkling conversation had so captivated him. Her eyes had been wet with tears as he had taken his leave and kissed her timidly on the cheek. In a burst of feeling he had turned about after a few steps toward the waiting carriage and, running back, had caught her up in his arms and kissed her fiercely on the lips.

The memory of that kiss filled his mind as the stage rumbled and jolted its way toward London. No other woman he had ever met had affected him so, leaving him filled with an ill-defined, unfulfilled longing.

Before he had traveled a dozen miles on his long journey south, the realization came to young William Howe De Lancey that he had fallen madly, hopelessly, in love.

2
The Rascal Army

IT MUST HAVE BEEN nearly noon before the first gun was fired. The roar of the cannon echoed and then re-echoed off the steep banks on each side of the river. Down at the quayside, it brought De Lancey up short, made him lift his head and glance about him apprehensively. Behind, the cliff rose precipitously to the walled stone terrace of the Serra Convent, where Sir Arthur and his staff were training their telescopes on the French positions opposite. In front, the gray reach of the great Douro River stretched across more than three hundred yards to the steep banks opposite. The morning mists had gradually burned off as the sun penetrated at last into the deep river canyon. From where De Lancey stood he could see clearly into the narrow streets of the town over there, already filled with clusters of red as the British infantry swarmed up to the fortress-like stone walls of the Bishop's Seminary. Beside him, another platoon of heavy-booted soldiers clumped down into the hold of the ancient wine barge lying alongside, easing themselves with furtive grins into the unfamiliar surroundings of this enormous wooden shoe, which reeked of the wine that was its normal cargo.

"Move along, move along; lively, now!" he called to the young subaltern shepherding his men down into the boat. Then he caught the eye of Colonel Waters, relaxing with his doughty little band of Portuguese on the end of the quay, and instantly his apprehensions vanished with the last of the morning mists. There was no mistaking the quiet triumph in the colonel's eyes, the broad grin that animated the sun-browned face beneath its battered shako.

"I think we've done it!" he called to De Lancey. "We must have more than six hundred men in the town already and the Frogs'll be too busy now to pay much attention to anything going on down here on the river."

"I believe you're right," responded De Lancey, grinning back at the colonel. "We put the Buffs into the seminary more than an hour ago, and the French will never get them out of there, now that they've had time to get stuck in."

Packed with troops, the heavy barge alongside was already pushing off from the stone quay, its sweating Portuguese crew rigging out the long sweeps that would take it across to add its human cargo to the British assault force that had gained so firm a foothold in the ancient town of Oporto, the strategic key to northern Portugal. Another barge was taking its place, its bluff, upturned bow nosing into the berth just vacated, its heavy timbers creaking as it eased alongside the stonework of the quay. De Lancey turned back to the job of overseeing the embarkation of yet another platoon, dark-uniformed Portuguese as well as British redcoats.

This furiously busy morning, May 12, 1809, was the culmination of weeks of concentrated activity, the most eventful and certainly the most demanding period of De Lancey's young life. After a stormy passage out in a man-o'-war, HMS *Surveillante*, he had arrived with Wellesley and a large staff at Lisbon on April 22, sailing up the Tagus past the white wedding-cake fortress at Belem to a tumultuous welcome at Black Horse Square, packed with wildly cheering Portuguese. It was Sir Arthur's mission to help these people drive the French from their country, and he had set about the task with his accustomed energy and efficiency. He had cut his stay in Lisbon, the beautiful, dirty Portuguese capital, to the barest minimum—De Lancey had only just learned how to find his way about the city (taking care to carry an umbrella at night to avoid the slops thrown into the streets from overhead windows) before he and the rest of the staff were hustled off to Coimbra to join the army already there.

It had taken just a week for Wellesley to hammer 17,000 British and 6,000 Portuguese into an effective allied force. He had, for the first time, organized it into divisions, each capable of acting autonomously under its own commander. He had firmed up the brave but raw Portuguese infantry by putting a battalion of them into each of five British brigades, and he had added to his army's skirmishing ability by giving each brigade a permanent company of riflemen, to protect it from the galling fire of the sharpshooting *voltigeurs*, which were such a feature of French tactics. As deputy quartermaster general, the brunt of all this dramatic reorganization had fallen upon De Lancey, and he had worked night and day, up to twenty hours in a single stretch, to complete the organization of what was to become the toughest and most efficient army in British history. A fortnight after landing in Portugal, Wellesley had his army on the march, moving northward into the wine-growing country and driving a sullen Soult, with a numerically stronger army, back to the French base established at Oporto, the old port city on the Douro River.

Later, on May 11, the tired British army camped for the night on the outskirts, high above the river opposite the city itself. At two o'clock the next morning it had been awakened by a tremendous explosion, a thunderous roar heard right across Portugal, as French sappers blew up the only bridge across the fast-flowing river. Satisfied that he had effectively isolated his fortress-city from any British interference, and ordering all barges and boats along the river to be collected on the waterfront under the protection of his guns, Marshal Soult retired to bed. But the Frenchmen assigned to the job had botched the roundup of boats. A young Portuguese barber in the town, anxious to join his friends in the allied army, had found a small skiff pulled up on the bank just outside the town and, while rowing across, had noticed four large wine barges tucked, unnoticed by the French, in a tiny cove hidden from above by an overhanging cliff. Arrived on the British side, the barber had encountered Colonel Waters, the daredevil head of the army's scouts, and had told him about the hidden barges. Waters could scarcely believe his luck; with his commander's approval he had set about rounding up a volunteer crew to bring the barges across. No Englishman would understand the handling of those great clumsy craft, propelled by enormous sweeps, but Waters had no difficulty collecting a crew of Portuguese all eager for the attempt: the barber, a prior, and four peasants.

To everyone's delighted surprise, the operation had gone without a hitch. Shrouded in morning mist, the barges had been sculled across, one after the other, without any interference from the sleeping French. De Lancey had organized the assault force into groups of thirty, that being the most the barges could be expected to accommodate without overloading, and had carefully handpicked the units that would form the first waves.

A company of the Third Foot, called The Buffs because of the facings of their uniform, and renowned for their steadiness under fire, had been first to cross, with orders from Wellesley to find their way up the steep streets of the town to the square, stone-walled Bishop's Seminary on the hilltop on the outskirts of town, which Sir Arthur had picked out as the key to the position. The Buffs quickly converted it into a veritable fortress. The British landings had continued, uninterrupted by any shot or shout from French sentinels; it was almost midday before the cannon shot indicated awareness of the assault on what had been considered an impregnable position.

But by then it was too late. The French launched a fierce attack on the seminary, but foundered before the concentrated firepower of its defenders. The long, rolling volleys, fired at command by disciplined troops from secure positions, shredded the attacking column, and, as the French recoiled, their disorder quickly grew to panic. Within minutes they were streaming out of the town on the roads leading north. Word of their straggling retreat was brought to Soult just as he sat down to breakfast. Catching up his sword, he galloped off with some of his staff to try to rally his broken army, but it was too late—it was impossible to restore order in the warren of narrow lanes and rutted streets. Accepting the inevitable, the disgruntled marshal rode out in the midst of his shaken forces, to rally and re-form them at their first halt on the highway to the north.

For Sir Arthur Wellesley and his new-forged allied army, it was victory, decisive and complete, and made all the sweeter for having been accomplished so quickly and at so little cost. With only a handful of casualties, the British and Portuguese found themselves masters of what had been reckoned to be one of the most difficult cities in the peninsula to assault. A morning's work had accomplished what a long and difficult siege might never have done. At four o'clock that afternoon Wellesley sat down to the meal that had been laid out for Marshal Soult only a short time earlier; he reported it to be one of the tastiest he had ever enjoyed.

For his elated troops there was a night of merrymaking as guests of the overjoyed populace of the liberated town. The Portuguese barber who had discovered the barges was the hero of the evening, and in British messes Colonel Waters was duly toasted by his comrades in arms. But for De Lancey the day had brought recognition of a different sort. Wellesley, famous for his quick eye in the field, had noted with approval the efficiency and speed with which his young staff officer had selected and organized the assault forces, displaying a capacity and understanding beyond his years. In his dispatches to London that evening, Sir Arthur, after lauding the exploit of Colonel Waters, had recommended his young deputy quartermaster general to the attention of the War Office. To be singled out for commendation by the ablest British general in the field was a great honor for the young soldier, and his first official recognition; it would not be his last.

In the long campaign that followed, marching and countermarching across the mountains and plains of Portugal and Spain for five wearying years, De Lancey wrote to Magdalene whenever he had a moment to himself. The letters had no real beginning or end, and were sent off whenever a dispatch leaving for England offered an opportunity. There was little in his letters of the actions fought; of battles lost and won. Mostly he wrote about the places visited, the tiny hill towns in the scorched mountains, the goats and fleas and burning sun, and of the men about him, his comrades in arms in this unique Peninsular Army.

They were, by any standards, a remarkable body of men, and to Magdalene, reading of them in her far-off Dunglass garden, they seemed more like creatures of myth and fantasy than the stolid Scots and Englishmen she was accustomed to. The men, from all accounts, were a hardbitten set of rascals; Irish Catholics, like the Connaught Rangers, brigaded with dour Highland Presbyterians, farm boys jostling with the scrapings of the London slums. But their officers seemed even more diverse—what was one to make of a general who went into action in a battered top hat, like "Daddy" Hill, or even a red nightcap, like Sir Thomas Picton? Her own De Lancey seemed surrounded by a wild set of young officers; he wrote about Dan Mackinnon, who had impersonated a nun at a convent being visited by Wellesley, and had once passed himself off as the Duke of York at a state banquet, where he had plunged headfirst into the punchbowl.

But what De Lancey's letters reflected, above all, was the growing efficiency and confidence of this remarkable army, the finest fighting force in Europe, and of its even more remarkable leader, who would become Viscount Wellington of Talavera after his crushing victory at that ancient Spanish city, but was known affectionately throughout the army as "Old Nosey" because of his prominent beak. Leader and army seemed to take on a common identity and reflect a common character: tough, plain, undemonstrative, inured to hardship, and with a wry, sardonic sense of humor which made light of difficulties. It was not a showy army; Wellington cared little about details of dress or drill, putting all emphasis on performance in the field. It was its superb steadiness under fire, its disciplined musketry, and its ability to absorb punishment without any loss of composure that made this army, over a five-year period, into a fighting machine that shook the world. One after another Bonaparte sent his best troops, his ablest marshals, against it. One after the other Wellington's army sent them stumbling back to France in defeat and humiliation: Junot, Soult, Victor, Massena, Marmont, Clausel, Souham, Jourdan. Operating at the end of a long, often tenuous, supply line stretching all the way back to England, and directed by penurious and vacillating politicians and bureaucrats, the army was constantly on the march, forced to live largely by its wits as alliances shifted and governments changed. Its progress had been marked by great victories—over Victor at Talavera, Massena at Bussaco and Fuentes, Marmont at Salamanca, Soult at Orthez and Toulouse—but Wellington showed himself as much a master in retreat as in victory.

Perhaps the greatest British triumph was the skilful withdrawal to their marvelously contrived lines of fortification at Torres Vedres. Stretching from the Tagus to the sea, they were so strong that Marshal Massena, led so carefully up the garden path, at sight of them could only raise his hat in rueful congratulation before leading his army, after weeks of starvation, on a long and ignominious retreat.

For young William De Lancey, the most memorable of all the long list of actions was the storming of Ciudad Rodrigo, the fortress on the Spanish-Portuguese border. Named for the Visigothic king whose tall tower atop a steep hill dominated the town at its foot, and elaborately fortified by the Moors and the medieval Christian kings, Ciudad Rodrigo was one of the strongest fortresses in Spain. It was approached by a magnificent Roman bridge across the Agueda, and its ancient defenses had been strengthened by modern additions and improvements. Massena had made it his principal base. On January 8, 1812, a small force of volunteers led by Colonel Colborne captured an outlying strongpoint overlooking the town in a daring attack, and from this dominating position, called the Great Teson, the British began their siege.

From the beginning it was a grim and desperate business. The British were forced to dig their approach ditches in frozen, snow-covered ground, under direct fire from the French batteries, using shoddy entrenching tools made of poor-quality steel by a profiteering contractor. Working night and day they brought their own guns to bear on the walls of the ancient fortress, and in ten days they managed to make two breaches in the outer defenses and bring their zigzag trenches to within assaulting range.

At seven o'clock on the evening of January 19, the attack began. Picton led the Third Division against one breach and Crawford's Light Division assaulted the other, supported by two minor attacks on the castle wall and the

Santiago Gate. It was the most ferocious attack yet undertaken by Wellington's army, and the men were like wolves after living for days in snow shelters on half rations.

Led by its "forlorn hope" of twenty-five men, all resigned to die, each storming party of 300 volunteers, committed to use of the bayonet only, went scrambling over heaps of fallen masonry toward the breaches, outlined by fire in the dark night. Concentrated French musketry and cannon fire mowed down many, and the enormous explosion of a mine, dug under the main breach and set off by the French, killed in a single instant the entire front rank of the attackers, but the survivors behind, maddened now by the deafening noise and slaughter, pressed on past the dreadful carnage of the crater. The assault was irresistible; in a matter of minutes the British had gained the breaches, bayoneted their immediate defenders, and put the rest to flight. Ciudad Rodrigo was theirs.

But if the assault had shown the British soldier at his best, the capture soon showed him at his worst. Jubilant parties of soldiers broke away from their units in search of plunder; in no time they had discovered, and broken into, large stores of liquor. In the twinkling of an eye a victorious, disciplined army became a drunken, disorderly mob, breaking into houses bent on rape and robbery, and even the best efforts of their officers could not deter them. The night was given over to drunken revelry, and many people, soldiers and civilians, women as well as men, were killed by random musketry. The men who marched out of the city the next morning were festooned with loot. Hams and bottles dangled from belts, silk dresses and furs were draped around necks, and almost all the soldiers had red-rimmed eyes set in throbbing heads.

It took a day of hard marching to work off the effects of the liquor, and the disciplinary measures of appalled regimental officers and furious non-commissioned officers to restore proper soldierly appearance to their units, but the excesses of Ciudad Rodrigo were a somber foretaste of worse things to come.

Yet for William De Lancey the disorders of the night could not rob the attacks of their triumph. Along with a number of other young officers, he had taken advantage of a special dispensation of their commander-in-chief, which allowed a few members of his staff to join a fighting unit for the assault. De Lancey had been in the forefront of a storming party that had carried one of the breaches in the wall, and had led his men with such dash and determination that Wellington had singled him out for special mention in a dispatch to London. It was the second such commendation from a general who was notoriously sparing of his praise, and it marked De Lancey's growing stature as both an able administrator and a first-class fighting soldier.

But Ciudad Rodrigo served merely as a preliminary to Badajoz. This immense border fortress, reputedly the strongest in Europe, had already withstood two previous sieges by the British when it was again invested by Wellington in 1812. Twenty days of hard digging and building and fighting had induced a sort of cold fury in the men toiling in the trenches. On the morning of the final assault British officers were struck by the strained, ferocious aspect of their men as they readied themselves, in silence, for the attack. "They looked at the walls above like tigers ravening for their prey," De Lancey was to recall.

At precisely ten o'clock of a black night, April 6, 1812— Easter Sunday, of all days—the tigers were let loose. The British attackers climbed the steep slopes in silence; in the misty darkness above they could hear the French sentries on the ramparts exchanging challenges: "*Sentinelle! Gardez-vous!*" The line of the storming parties had reached the crest, and was standing on the lip of the deep ditch directly in front of the tumbled masonry of the breaches in the wall, when a French fireball soared into the air high overhead, its brilliance illuminating everything on both sides in vivid detail, just before the moment of impact. From their wall, the defenders could see long lines of attackers, rank upon rank, like waves of steel rising toward them, but it was the British who were appalled by what they saw before them. The ditch, which had been filled with rubble from the gaps smashed in the wall by British artillery, had been cleared by the defenders, working under cover of darkness. At the bottom of the ten-foot ditch were tangles of iron-spiked obstructions of every sort and buried mines. Tar barrels were now set alight and tumbled from the walls. Chains had been drawn across the gaps in the wall, thick planks with metal spikes a foot long barred the way up from the ditch, and, most terrible of all, enormous beams of timber, set with hundreds of sword blades and chained to the wall, spanned each breach at the summit.

It was a ghastly sight, but it seemed only to raise the fury of the attackers to a new pitch, and with a roared "Hurrah!" they threw themselves into the assault. Planks were brought to span the ditch, and lines of men teetered precariously above the moat, only to be swept away by the French musketry. From the walls above, barrels of gunpowder were trundled down to explode in the ditch, killing and maiming scores of attackers. Mines, dug in the bottom, were set off by powder trains, their explosions hurling dozens of flailing bodies high into the night sky. Yet still the British surged forward. Those behind pushed those in front into the ditch, where they strove to ascend the far bank on makeshift ladders or by climbing on the shoulders of their comrades. Here and there small parties gained the crest, only to fall victim to the horrors of the *chevaux de frise*, whose sword blades were soon heavy with bodies, spiked and spitted by the pressure of the attackers.

To those in the rear ranks of the assault, the breaches

in the wall appeared like so many rivers of fire as French guns and muskets poured devastation into the ranks of the attackers, exploding now and then like volcanoes as some mine or powder barrel was touched off in the ditch.

It was a night of sustained horror, without precedent in European warfare. Forty times the British bugles sounded the attack, and forty times fresh waves went forward with loud "Hurrahs," only to fill the ditch with dead and dying. Among the first to fall was Captain Francis Gwillim Simcoe, the twenty-one-year-old son of Colonel John Graves Simcoe. To De Lancey, at Wellington's side on a hillock overlooking the scene, the breaches, filled with flame and tumult, seemed like the gates of hell. It was the noise that was most daunting; the agonized shrieks of the wounded and the shouts of the attackers provided a dreadful counterpoint to the thunder of the cannonade, the explosions, and the musketry. And at the end of an hour of sustained fighting the British seemed no further ahead, for all their outpouring of blood in those frightful breaches. Even the imperturbable Wellington had turned pale and allowed his chin to sag when the failure of the assault on the breaches became apparent.

But what had been planned as merely a subsidiary attack, an escalade on the walls of the citadel itself, had, against all the odds, succeeded where the main attacks had failed. Climbing long ladders propped against the high castle walls, and despite heavy losses as ladders were pushed away or their climbers shot by defenders, volunteers from Picton's Third and Leith's Fifth divisions had pressed home their attack with such dash and gallantry that they had been able to establish a foothold atop the wall; a foothold which, once secured, grew rapidly until the British had seized control of the rampart top and then, ultimately, of the citadel itself.

In moments the defenders were streaming in panic away

from the walls, and a wave of jubilant British soldiers attacked the French at the breaches from behind. Minutes later, the whole fortress was in British hands, and thousands of British soldiers, maddened by the horror of the breaches and drunk with fighting frenzy, poured into the streets and squares of the town. The most terrible assault in the history of the British army was to be crowned by the most terrible sack.

A sort of communal madness seized the troops streaming into the deserted, narrow streets. They had been tried past endurance by their ordeal in the breaches and the ditch, and were now beyond all controlling. The shattering scenes they had witnessed—five thousand of them had died in the most frightful manner under those walls, and many more had been torn and mangled, burned and maimed, on those unspeakable barriers—had turned them into a troop of demons, raging for revenge. Every door was kicked in, every house sacked; the women were raped, the helpless shot or bayoneted. No one was spared, not even old men, infants, or invalids.

Here and there a few acts of mercy, of heroism even, lightened the blackness. A young infantry officer, Sir Harry Smith, rescued a young girl of fourteen, her ears bleeding where her earrings had been torn off, from a drunken band. (She was to survive to become his wife, Lady Smith, and give her name to a town in South Africa.)

No one was safe from the armed mob that roamed the streets that night, not even the British soldiers themselves. Many were killed in brawls over plunder, still others by random shooting. Officers who ventured to interfere, to restore some form of discipline, were butchered on the spot. Wellington himself, riding into town, narrowly avoided death from a random shot fired by a celebrating soldier.

The army was completely out of hand. All through that

dreadful night drunken soldiers caroused and butchered and looted. Often a house that had been thoroughly plundered would have its remaining furnishings piled up and set on fire in a senseless orgy of destruction. But, unlike Ciudad Rodrigo, there was no cessation of the rioting once the awful night had passed. Dawn broke on a town in its death throes, on a mob of drunken, maddened men who now fell to fighting one another. The British army was in danger of melting away. Already deserters, laden with loot, were stealing off in twos and threes from the smoking town. Wellington, who had actually broken down and wept when he visited the breaches in the morning and saw the carnage there, where five thousand of his finest soldiers lay dead in heaps, attempted to restore the men to their senses by issuing a general order: "It is full time that the plunder of Badajoz should cease."

When this failed to stem the lawlessness, he took sterner action on the following day, April 8. A working party of steady men was sent into the town under the Provost Marshal. They set up a row of gallows, sixteen in all, on the ground beneath the grim cathedral walls. Non-commissioned officers from the various regiments, accompanied by drummers and buglers, were sent round the streets of the town, sounding the "Fall-in" and rousing every man they could find out into the street.

The greater part of the army had already returned to the colors, and they were drawn up now, in a hollow square, facing the cathedral and the row of gibbets. After the sergeants had returned, bringing with them most of the missing men, and had pushed them into place in the ranks of their regiments, a solitary party of buglers and drummers was sent around the town, again sounding the "Fall-in" for the benefit of any late stragglers. Five minutes after they had returned, the "Bloody Provost" took over. Patrols of burly soldiers were sent into the streets, looking into every house or cellar that might still shelter army fugitives, now officially classified as deserters. They returned, dragging scores of drunken, fighting men, who were lined in straggling queues behind each gallows.

The executions began while fresh deserters were still being brought in; sixteen men had nooses placed about their necks and were hauled aloft, to dangle there until they had choked to death. The shaken regiments watched as the first sixteen men were lowered lifeless, to be trundled into a pit dug in the ground behind, and their places taken by another sixteen. The second lot were snatched aloft, to dance in the air, and even the most hard-bitten old campaigners in the watching ranks looked on with pale, set faces.

After the second lot had been dispatched, Wellington allowed himself to be dissuaded from further executions by the intervention of a group of his divisional commanders. On their assurance that the men had learned their lesson, and could be relied upon never to fall into such disorderly riot again, the remaining deserters were granted their lives, merely receiving a flogging before being allowed to rejoin their regiments.

Tough though these soldiers might be, they had learned the hard way that they were commanded by an even tougher leader, a taciturn, hawk-nosed general who would soon become known throughout Europe as the "Iron Duke."

"The great adventure," as De Lancey described the long Iberian campaign, ended on the banks of the Zadorra River, not far from the Spanish town of Vitoria, which gave its name to the battle. Here, in 1813, on a hilltop where the Black Prince had led his English knights to glory centuries before, Wellington's British and Portuguese regiments, vying with one another in dash and gallantry, had crushed a French army led by Joseph Bonaparte himself, the self-made King of Spain. The victory, the culminating triumph of the whole Peninsular campaign, was followed by the anticlimax of low comedy, when British light cavalry intercepted a French baggage train which included

Joseph's own coach. The king was forced to flee on the back of one of his escort's horses, leaving behind his silver monogrammed chamber pot, bundles of perfumed love letters, and a fortune in stolen Spanish paintings and bullion. The baggage train included hundreds of gaily dressed women, together with their wardrobes, jewelry, and pet dogs and monkeys: "an ambulatory brothel," as it was described to De Lancey by a laughing young hussar officer whose regiment had been assigned to guard it after its capture.

Vitoria marked the end of Bonaparte's attempt to rule Spain as a sort of family kingdom. Henceforth the French were to conduct a protracted withdrawal northward and eastward to their own borders, hounded and harried by Wellington's victorious army.

For De Lancey himself, Vitoria was of particular significance. His eye for choosing effective positions, his dash, and his energy in enabling the army to march four hundred miles in forty days, won him another mention in Wellington's dispatches, but, more importantly, it secured him a new posting as deputy quartermaster general to Sir Thomas Graham, Wellington's second-in-command. In his new post, De Lancey became the trusted adviser and confidant of this amiable and experienced old soldier. It was his duty to draw up his order of battle, listing the units available and their position and condition. He helped his commander to select and inspect prospective fields of battle, and, once they were chosen, to issue the marching orders that would put individual units in their proper place at the right time. It was a complex and highly responsible position, requiring a detailed knowledge of maps and country and character, and De Lancey reveled in it.

The long list of allied successes continued to unroll: the capture, after an initial check, of San Sebastian; the crossing of the Bidassoa into France; the passage, after a sharp action, of the Nivelle and then the Nive; the victories over Soult at Orthez and Toulouse.

During a grand dinner at the Prefecture in Toulouse on April 12, 1814, official word was brought to Wellington by a travel-stained messenger on a foam-flecked horse: Napoleon had abdicated! The war to rid Europe of the great tyrant was ended.

Wellington stood up and announced his momentous news to an awed audience. Bonaparte had fallen, was banished to Elba; King Louis XVIII now ruled in his place. In the tumultuous rejoicing that broke out afterward, De Lancey took particular pleasure in drinking the toast proposed by the gallant Spanish general Alava to his "friend and comrade" Wellington as "*El Liberador de España!*"

In truth, it had been a remarkable accomplishment, this expulsion of the French tyrant from the Iberian peninsula and the liberation of Spain and Portugal; to De Lancey it had been a kind of crusade. But in the early hours of the morning, as the revelry wound down, he could not help wondering what was to become of this remarkable army. All these roistering comrades-in-arms about him, these brother officers still so young in years yet old in experience: what would they do? War was their trade, they knew nothing else. Like De Lancey, they had been born and nurtured in what seemed an endless time of war; peace was something beyond their experience. It was a thoughtful De Lancey who finally sought his bed as dawn reddened the eastern sky.

In the event, the army simply melted away. In the weeks that followed, after its leader departed for Paris and the weighty affairs of state that awaited him there, the army shrank day by day, as regiment after regiment departed from Bordeaux and the transport ships that would carry them to their next posting. Some regiments were sent off to North America, others to India or the West Indies, but most were bound for England or Ireland and inevitable demobilization. Even the best, the most experienced, units, toughened and tempered by years of hard fighting in Iberia, were broken up, a few of their officers put on half-pay and everyone else "turned out to starve," as some complained bitterly.

But for De Lancey the first postwar weeks brought a surprise that wiped out all doubts and misgivings about the future. In Paris, en route home, an official communication from London notified him that he had been appointed, by the Prince Regent's order, a Knight Companion of the Order of the Bath. Henceforth he was Sir William De Lancey, a distinction he owed to the good opinion of Wellington himself. For a young American officer with no influence at court or in high government circles, it represented a rare honor and a notable achievement. He was just thirty-two years old, with no permanent employment, nor prospect of any, but when he arrived back in England in the summer of 1814 he was flushed with a sense of achievement and filled with a consuming eagerness and hope. For his sole purpose was clear, overriding all other considerations: he was determined to make Magdalene Hall his wife.

3
Magdalene!

FOR AN IMPATIENT young man with a mission, London in 1814 proved a sore trial. The capital, like all European cities, was caught up in a wave of postwar euphoria that had transformed official life from its usual wartime drudgery to a seemingly endless round of balls and receptions and revels of one sort or another. Even the unpopular war in America was forgotten in the dizzying spectacle of a world at peace, free from the tyranny of the megalomaniac now playing out his life as king of the island of Elba, complete with a miniature army and a toy navy. True, London was full of romantics like Byron, who idealized the exiled Napoleon as an eagle encaged, and of pessimistic politicians who doubted that the fat and fatuous Bourbon now installed as Louis XVIII could capture the fancy of a French nation accustomed to domination of the world, but these were of minor concern to a capital conscious of having led Europe to a great victory in a long and arduous war, and determined to enjoy itself.

From the moment he arrived, after posting up from Portsmouth, De Lancey found himself caught up in a round of occasions, both public and private, that demanded his attendance. There was no escape; as a senior staff officer to the man who was now regarded as the savior of the country and the foremost man in Europe, De

Lancey was very much in demand. There were dozens of official duties to be performed at the Horse Guards, and endless official receptions and banquets. It was pleasant to receive the ribbon and star of The Order of the Bath from the hands of the Prince Regent, beaming and benevolent at the investiture, and full of kind words at the reception afterward, but the crowded, overheated rooms, the rich food, the late hours, and the fulsome flattery made a life of indulgence more of a penance than a pleasure.

For De Lancey, it was a relief when his official army duties were at last terminated, and he was allowed to escape, a half-pay officer on indefinite leave, from the cloying capital. He caught the first stage to the north, and rattled out of a midnight London without a backward look.

The trip north seemed interminable, hour after jolting hour in the stuffiness of the coach, broken by snatched meals in chilly coffee rooms as the horses were changed. At York he had moved to an outside seat, hoping for some refreshing air and relief from the dismal confinement of the interior, but out on the moors the weather had changed for the worse, and he was soon soaked through by the persistent rain and wind. Mile after dreary mile he sat huddled in his wet topcoat, sleepless and aching in every joint, as the ancient vehicle rumbled and rattled its way northward over the rutted road.

But if the trip had proved to be purgatory, arrival was pure heaven. A watery sun emerged as the stage clattered into the outskirts of Edinburgh, and as it drew up at the staging inn in a lather of sweat and shouting, there in the little huddle of waiting passengers and ostlers was the beaming face of old Sir James Hall, and there beside him—oh, heaven indeed!—was Magdalene, radiant as any angel. All discomfort, all weariness, were swept away in a rapturous welcome of handshakes and embraces, and they were off in the Hall carriage for the short ride to Dunglass.

The days that followed blurred into a single dreamlike sequence for the travel-worn De Lancey. There was sleep, for one thing—ten hours at a stretch, that first night— deep, dreamless, restoring. There was talk, too, endless talk, for there was so much to catch up on. All his Spanish adventures had to be recounted, for Sir James was a careful, sometimes a demanding, listener, and opinions had to be expressed on all De Lancey's comrades in arms, from Picton to Packenham to Murray and the great Sir Arthur himself. Even the little incidents of campaign life were eagerly sought out by Sir James; he especially relished the camaraderie that developed between the old stagers of the British army and their French counterparts, and he laughed at De Lancey's account of the pickets of the two armies, separated only by a narrow Spanish river, who used to share the same tobacco pouch, flung back and forth across the stream.

"They became so friendly that when one or other army was planning an attack next morning its picket would shout across to the other: 'Take care of yourself tomorrow!' " said De Lancey, laughing.

But, most of all, there was Magdalene. She seemed to have blossomed since De Lancey had last seen her. The shy young girl was now a mature and beautiful woman with dark, lustrous eyes, auburn hair swept up from a slender neck in the new fashion, and a delicate complexion set off by soft, full lips just meant for kissing, De Lancey was sure. She dressed in demure fashions that yet contrived to show off trim ankles and a bewitching figure that gave no mercy to a young man already head over heels in love.

The two talked endlessly. They had been close to begin with; their letters, over the long time apart, had bridged the physical gap, and reflected both the growing maturity of their new adulthood and the intimacy of mutual trust and understanding.

They were, by any standard, a remarkable pair. Magdalene, for all her sheltered provincial background, showed a grasp of world affairs and an understanding of human nature that deeply impressed De Lancey. Her sensitivity, humor, and, above all, great strength of character made her a woman unlike any other he had ever met, a world away from the chattering creatures he was accustomed to in fashionable London circles.

For her part, Magdalene was enchanted with her William. Behind the dynamic soldier and young man of the world she sensed, and loved, the imaginative, dreamy romantic, sweet-tempered and hungry for affection.

From the beginning it was apparent that the two were made for each other, and it was no surprise to Sir James when, one evening after dinner, he was asked by his young house guest for his daughter's hand in marriage. De Lancey, it appeared, had proposed to Magdalene in the little summerhouse after an afternoon walk, and had been accepted; Sir James's blessing, so anxiously asked, was heartily given.

The Golden Fleece was not a pretentious-looking hostelry. It had a plain limestone front, high and narrow, with small windows looking at the terraced houses across the cobbled street, but for the newly married couple it was the face of paradise. On a quiet cul-de-sac just off the Canongate in Edinburgh, the old inn, known for its comfort and good food, was where the De Lanceys had elected to spend their honeymoon, and its landlord had given them his best accommodation, a pair of rooms across the front of the building on the second floor.

The late-April wedding in the little stone church at Dunglass, the reception at the Hall afterward, the cloud of friends and family and well-wishers, the kisses and handshakes, and the rowdy send-off were a memory now, part of that other, outside world left behind on the drive into the city. Here, in this warm and private place they shared, dream had become reality, and life together a prospect of infinite happiness.

They were a striking couple, and they drew admiring attention wherever they went in the ancient stone-built city. Even in civilian clothes, De Lancey caught the eye—his handsome face and figure, the animation of his manner and conversation, stood out in any company—but it was the charm and beauty of his young wife that won all hearts, and enchanted the sophisticated society in which the young couple found themselves.

The two were obviously deeply in love. Fashionable Edinburgh quickly recognized that neither of these two dazzling newcomers in its midst had much time or attention to spare from their mutual adoration of one another, and accordingly left them largely to themselves.

But the idyll was not to last. On the evening of the tenth day of their marriage, the De Lanceys heard the news that had arrived from London and soon set all Edinburgh agog. Napoleon had ended his brief exile in Elba and had landed in southern France. Ney, his old marshal, had left Paris at the head of an army, promising King Louis to bring back Bonaparte "in an iron cage," but when he came face to face with his old leader, Ney's resolution had melted in sentimental tears. He, and his army with him, had yielded to Napoleon's blandishments and had marched northward with their intended prisoner. Napoleon was even now in Paris at the head of a large and growing army, as his old soldiers, weary of a flaccid Bourbon monarchy which seemed to have learned nothing from its long years of exile, flocked to their Emperor's banner. The king had fled, and all Europe was again in turmoil.

The news struck De Lancey like a blow in the face. As a professional soldier, he was once again to be caught up in the seemingly endless war against the Corsican. At the very moment of their greatest happiness, he and his lovely Magdalene were to be torn apart. It was almost too cruel to bear. Yet his duty was clear: they must return to Dunglass, the address where his superiors expected him to be, and where official news and orders could reach him. Beset by foreboding and fear, the young couple returned to the Hall home they had left only days before amid such happiness, and waited anxiously for word from London.

It was not long in coming. On the morning of the second day following their return, a young orderly officer arrived with an envelope he had brought direct from the Horse Guards offices of the commander-in-chief. Wellington had been named to command the allied European and British armies already assembling in Belgium, and he had selected De Lancey especially to be his quartermaster general, his principal aide and staff officer. Accompanying this announcement was another: De Lancey was promoted to the rank of colonel!

For a young officer, still only thirty-four years old, the promotion and appointment constituted a striking and singular honor, especially as Wellington had made the appointment a condition of his own acceptance of the post of commander-in-chief. But from a personal point of view the news was something less than welcome. He was summarily ordered to leave, without an hour's delay, to join his commander-in-chief in Brussels, to take up his new duties there at the headquarters of the Allied armies. Within the hour the young lover and husband of less than two weeks was once again on the road to London, Brussels, and the war.

In that lovely spring of 1815, Brussels found itself the capital of the fashionable world. Everyone who was anyone was there; London society seemed to have transferred itself, en masse, to the Belgian capital. Most of them, of course, had traveled there from Paris and other parts of Europe, where they had been renewing the pleasures of continental living after the long hiatus of the Napoleonic wars, seeking safety after Bonaparte's return and the flight of the Bourbon court, but a number of the most fashionable London hostesses had moved their salons to Brussels because of the presence there of Lord Wellington, and of his staff, which included many of Europe's foremost noblemen.

The Duchess of Richmond, whose family were longtime friends of the Wellesleys, had rented a house in the fashionable Rue de la Blanchisserie. Here Wellington occasionally dropped in for a meal or a romp with the Richmond children, and other aspiring hostesses soon established themselves as best they could in rented quarters nearby, where they hoped to attract a Prussian princeling, or at least a general officer, to one of their soirées.

Wellington had established his headquarters in Brussels because it was the strategic center of the Allied position, with good lines of communication through Antwerp to Britain, whence came his supplies and reinforcements. It was also the capital of Belgium, whose allegiance to the Allied cause was suspect, to put it mildly. Belgium had been part of the French empire for twenty years, and might easily revert to its old allegiance now that the Emperor had returned to Paris. Already French agents were at work, distributing leaflets reminding the Belgians of their share in past Napoleonic glories. To Wellington's mind, the surest way of keeping Belgium loyal was to establish an Allied army there. As Napoleon assembled his veterans in Paris, Wellington set up his headquarters in a number of rented houses fronting on a square that Brussels natives called simply "the park." It was here, on the fourth floor of a house belonging to the Count de Lannoy, that De

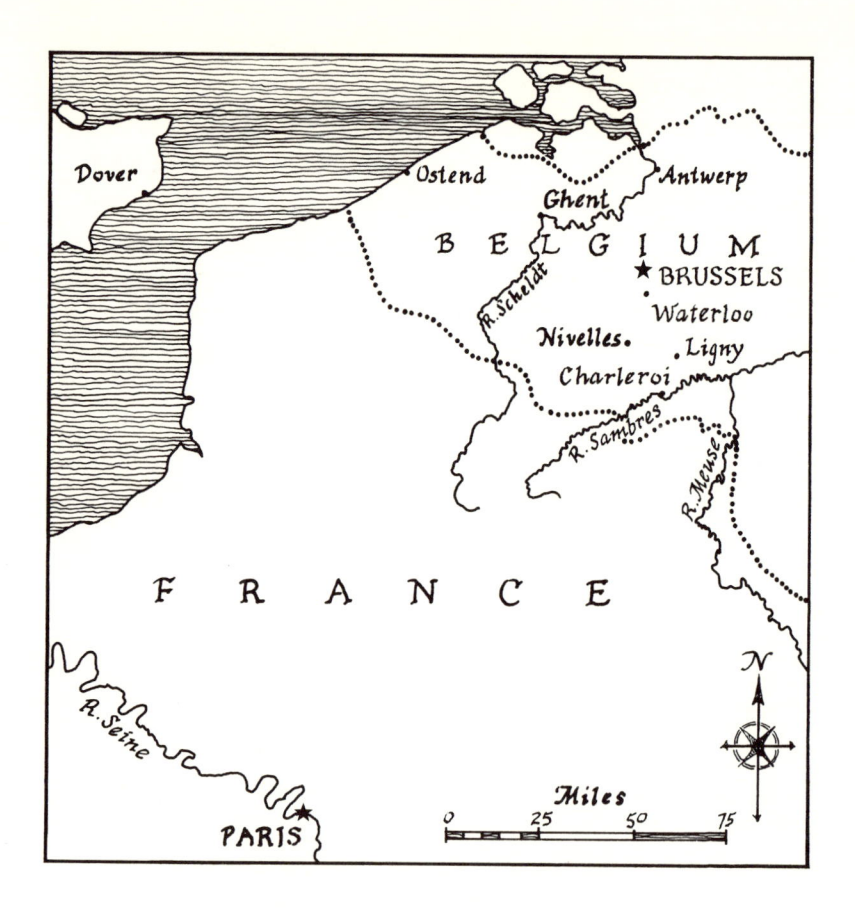

France and Belgium, 1815

Lancey found himself billeted, across the road from his ground-floor office as quartermaster general of the Allied Forces.

He had no sooner arrived, after a stormy Channel crossing, than he was summoned to a long interview with Wellington during which they examined Belgian maps in detail, and discussed the forces available. That discussion, enlivened as usual by the Duke's forthright comments, was enlightening if not entirely encouraging.

The Allied forces were strung out in an arc roughly parallel to the French border, from the Channel coast on the west to the Prussian border to the east. Many regiments were billeted in or near Brussels itself, while the Prussian army covered the eastern sector. All were located on good east-west highways, so as to be able to concentrate quickly once Napoleon's intentions were known, for until he sallied forth across the border his actions were technically a matter of French domestic politics.

Wellington, aware of his own dependence on Antwerp as the key to his communications with Britain, expected that Napoleon would attempt to strike quickly along the Channel coast to cut Brussels off from the sea and to encourage the Belgians to rise against the Allied army in their midst. Until he had intelligence of French intentions, however, he intended to keep his army deployed along Belgium's excellent road system and avoid a premature concentration that might play into Bonaparte's hands.

De Lancey found himself dealing with an army far different from the British troops he was accustomed to. There were units, like some of the Netherlander and Saxony regiments, whose allegiance to the Allied cause was doubtful at best, and there were many more collections of raw conscripts whose loyalty might be unquestioned but whose fighting value was not of the highest. The Prussian army, operating as a separate entity under the command of Marshal Blücher, a rough illiterate but a competent and loyal soldier, and General Gneisenau, his clever but unreliable chief of staff, was the single largest Allied force. In all, the Allied commanders had at their disposal a total force of 210,000 men with which to confront Napoleon's 122,000 veterans, but in reality they could count on an effective fighting force of approximately 120,000 men to cover the French frontier, split into Blücher's Prussian army and Wellington's Anglo-Dutch force. Blücher and Wellington had already met and discussed their common strategy; each committed himself to come to the other's aid if attacked.

The real strength of the Allied army lay in a British contingent of 33,000 men, of whom only some 7,000 infantry were seasoned veterans. The rest were raw, untried regiments, youngsters fresh from the plow for the most part, but already disciplined to the dour endurance and steadiness for which British infantry had become noted. These were the troops on which Wellington must rely to bear the brunt of any French attack in the forthcoming battle, and their disposition in the Allied line was De Lancey's principal preoccupation.

The Allied cavalry was a mixed blessing. On the one hand, the British and German horse regiments were magnificently mounted and equipped, and possessed of great spirit and dash, but offsetting their bravery and panache was the notorious tendency of British cavalry to lose control and cohesion after a charge, so that they were liable to fragment into a mere mounted rabble after a spirited charge pressed home too valiantly, and to be cut up by a countercharge. This was in notable contrast to the nimble French cavalry, accustomed to sustaining more maneuverable, if less furious, assaults.

The housing and feeding of these large numbers of men and horses was a major problem. De Lancey concentrated as many as possible in or about Brussels itself, the largest urban center in the country and the best able to cope with the needs of a large army, but the rest had to be scattered in small towns and villages for miles around, wherever billets could be found or food was available. Time would be needed to concentrate this scattered force and bring it to the field of battle, and for this essential advance notice Wellington was dependent on an elaborate intelligence network to keep him posted on the movements of French armies and, most important of all, of Napoleon himself. Until the emperor moved, Wellington could not commit himself.

There was certainly no shortage of reports. A swarm of Allied spies in France and casual correspondents everywhere kept the headquarters inundated with sightings and suggestions of every sort. Napoleon was at the border, an invasion of Belgium could be expected at any moment; Napoleon was in Paris and intended to remain there. A large French army was on the march eastward; all French troops were being concentrated in the north. Napoleon wanted war; he would sue for peace. He was bent on instant action; he was playing for time. Trying to sort out the welter of conflicting rumors and reports was an endless, and largely fruitless, task, and kept De Lancey and the rest of Wellington's staff in constant turmoil and anxiety.

There were other worries as well; one of Blücher's Saxon regiments was in open mutiny, and there were other rumblings of treachery and desertion from the east. De Lancey did not trust Gneisenau, and found that Wellington shared his doubts about the reliability of the Prussian chief of staff, but counted on Blücher to keep his shifty subordinate in line and his restless regiments under control. There were endless details to be attended to, a thousand matters for worry or concern, so it was a harried quartermaster general who responded with a testy "Come in!" to a tap on his door on the morning of June 8.

And suddenly, unbelievably, Magdalene was in his

arms, her wind-chilled cheek against his, the fragrance of her hair drowning his senses. Accompanied by Emma, her maid, she had made her way south to London, she explained between kisses, and had managed to get passage in a crowded packet brig to Antwerp on the Belgian coast, and then by stage to Brussels. Emma had been dreadfully seasick and was only now recovering, but her mistress was in good health and marvelous spirits at being reunited with her husband. Nothing else mattered, now that they were together again, she whispered, and her young husband murmured agreement as he pressed her close. The cares that had so beset him seemed mere trifles, to be sorted out with ease in a moment or two, now that this intoxicating woman was in his arms. With Magdalene by his side he felt he could accomplish anything, and he carried her off to be installed in his—now their—lodgings in the upper story of de Lannoy's house.

The week that followed was the most intense either had ever known; it was as if all their life together was to be compressed within the confines of a few days. De Lancey spent his days with orderlies and staff officers, moving the armies that would shape the future of Europe; the evenings were gay with balls and receptions, as if Europe were determined to dance the fateful hours away. The De Lanceys never went to any of the revels; they preferred to spend their evenings quietly, savoring the intimacy that had been so long denied them, and by common consent the Brussels hostesses honored their privacy, to allow these two charming young people to enjoy their own company without distraction.

For the fearful peoples of Britain, of Europe, it was a time of anxious waiting; for the armies, it was a time of feverish preparation. For the De Lanceys, it was a time of utter happiness, far beyond anything either had ever known, the culmination of their young lives.

It came to an end with shattering abruptness. On the afternoon of Thursday, June 15, while Wellington, De Lancey, and several other members of the Allied staff were dining in Brussels with the Spanish ambassador, General Alava, a Prussian officer, covered with dust and dirt and sweat, burst into the room. He had been sent by Blücher, and he bore momentous news. Napoleon had crossed the border into Belgium at Charleroi before dawn that morning, and was marching eastward, driving the Prussian cavalry pickets before him.

The news was not unexpected. For the past three days De Lancey had noticed that no communications had come from agents in France, no stagecoaches or individual riders had been allowed to cross the frontier. Obviously something was brewing on the border, and he had so informed his commander.

Wellington had no sooner digested the news and mentioned to his host, Alava, that he would have to cut short his meal and depart for headquarters than there was a further interruption. The young Prince of Orange, who had been given command of a small Allied force far to the west, arrived, pulled out a chair, and sat down to deliver his shattering news. The Prussians had been driven out of the villages they held all along the road leading into the heart of Belgium, and the French were even now well past Charleroi, directly south of Brussels and between the Anglo-Dutch army there and the Prussian army at Ligny. Napoleon, moving with surprising speed, was threatening to drive a wedge between Wellington and Blücher, and to defeat them individually before they could concentrate their numerically superior forces.

The Prince of Orange suddenly found himself the only one still seated; to a man, everyone else had scrambled to his feet as soon as the Prince had blurted out his news. He, too, rose when Wellington laid a hand on his shoulder with a muttered "Come with me!" and in a matter of seconds Alava's pleasant dinner party had disintegrated and his guests were galloping off to their various posts.

Before he left the room, De Lancey engaged in a brief low-voiced conversation with Wellington; then the Duke slapped his confidant on the shoulder and sent him on his way with an encouraging "You know what must be done!"

De Lancey arrived at his lodgings in the square with his horse in a lather, flung the reins to the orderly at the door, and dashed to his desk, which had been moved up to his rooms. He had a kiss and a brief explanation for a startled Magdalene, who promised to make herself scarce and not say a word, before he went to work. He must send out the orders that would set the Allied army in motion; orders that would tell each regiment the time it must set out, and the route it must follow to bring it to the field of battle on time. Despite the pressure of time, his orders must be clear and concise, must bring Napoleon to battle on Allied terms. On his shoulders now depended the fate of Europe, and he was fully aware of his responsibilities as he began to write.

He had no sooner started than he was interrupted by an urgent message from his commander-in-chief: Come at once! With a questioning glance at his wife, De Lancey left the room and hastened across the square to the Duke's lodgings, where he found the great man standing in dressing gown and slippers, in urgent conversation with an enormously fat officer whom the Duke introduced as General Muffling, an envoy from Marshal Blücher.

As soon as De Lancey arrived, Wellington took him aside in his dressing room. "Blücher has picked the fattest man in his army to ride with an express to me, and he has taken thirty hours to go thirty miles!" the Duke confided. Nonetheless, the news was useful. Blücher intended to stand at Ligny, and Wellington had determined to advance as far as Quatre Bras, the crossroads of the main east-west and north-south highways, to maintain touch with Blücher and await further news of French movements. Accordingly, a reserve of 20,000 men under Wellington himself would set out for Quatre Bras from Brussels at five o'clock in the morning. In the meantime the Duke would attend the Duchess of Richmond's ball planned for that evening, in order to allay rumor and panic among the civilian population. The dispositions already set in train by De Lancey would stand, concentrating the army at selected positions along the high ground between Nivelles and Quatre Bras.

From her window across the square, Magdalene watched anxiously for her husband's reappearance, wondering what emergency could have arisen to interrupt his urgent business. It seemed ages ago that she had pinned his medals and crosses on his dress uniform coat, and straightened his stock before sending him out to attend the Spanish ambassador's dinner. He had not wanted to go, preferring a quiet meal with her before their cosy fireside, but she knew that it was important that he be at the Duke's side at so important a function, attended by the chief officers of the army, and she had sent him off reluctantly, watching from her window as he rode out of sight. Now she was watching from the same window, conscious of the new and frightening circumstances and of the heavy load of responsibility that lay on her husband's young shoulders. It was a relief when she saw him reappear, and hasten across to their lodgings. She ran to meet him at the door.

4

After the Ball

There was a sound of revelry by night—
                                        Byron

ALL EVENING the carriages had been pouring through the square; first a trickle, later, as night drew on, a veritable stream, as the famous and the fashionable made their way to the great house rented by the Duchess of Richmond in the nearby Rue de la Blanchisserie. From her window high above the square, Magdalene watched them passing by, glimpsing ladies in shimmering silks and plumes and men in gold-laced uniforms of scarlet, blue, or green. The Duchess had chosen this night for her ball only after being assured by the Duke of Wellington himself that there would be no military operation to interrupt it, and she could not guess how nearly events had transpired to make him break his promise. But he had promised to attend, and attend he did, with every officer who could be spared from his immediate duties, arriving fashionably late to a scene of extraordinary opulence.

The Duchess, conscious of her responsibilities as the senior chatelaine in a city filled with notables of every sort from every capital in Europe, had not stinted in her arrangements. The house, ablaze with enormous chandeliers, had been transformed into a series of stunning settings for her glittering guests, as they arrived for what was to become the most famous ball in history.

From the open door, light and music poured into the street outside, which was jammed with coaches and carriages. Hostlers and drivers shouted and swore at their refractory horses as gorgeously dressed ladies and their equally splendid escorts made their way up the broad steps. Inside, each room had been transformed into the likeness of a magnificent pavilion, the ceilings tented in shimmering draperies and the pillars wreathed in rosettes and streamers of silk ribbon. In the main hall, a fountain played beneath an immense chandelier, and the ballroom, occupying almost the whole ground floor, had been transformed into a sort of summer palace, with rose-trellised walls and silk hangings of gold, crimson, and black, the Belgian royal colors. Bowls of roses filled the air with their perfume, and above the sound of voices, conversing in every tongue in Europe, rose the swell of the orchestra recruited from the Brussels opera house.

Into this opulent pleasure dome was crowded all that was fairest and best in Brussels society, along with every notable name among the hundreds of visitors to the city. Heading the list was His Royal Highness, the Prince of Orange, who Wellington considered should have been at his post near the French border but who had been unable to resist the opportunity of presiding over an affair of this magnitude. Every ambassador, general officer, and aristocrat in the city was there, along with all the dashing young officers from the regiments billeted in or near the capital, many of them aristocrats of high rank. For them, and for the young ladies already exchanging glances with them over their fans, the Duchess's ball promised to be an evening of memorable enjoyment, but for Wellington, already moving about the fringes of the ballroom, it was entirely a matter of business. Here were gathered all the officers and officials with whom he desired to speak about the great events he knew were now unfolding, and one by one he touched their shoulders or caught their eye and drew them aside for instruction or consultation. One or two were even dispatched to distant duties, taking hurried leave of their hostess before departing into the night, but most went back to the dancing, albeit with a thoughtful aspect. The Duke overlooked no one; even Napoleon's spy, a French general who attended the ball disguised in the uniform of a Belgian officer, found himself shaking hands with the Duke, who, noting the Belgian uniform, said merely: "We shall have sharp work soon. I am glad to see you."

At intervals, while the musicians refreshed themselves, guests were entertained by displays of Scottish dancing by men from the Highland regiments, who performed the intricate reels that had been made fashionable in London by the Prince Regent, their gaily flying kilts and plaids oddly at contrast with their fierce beards and dour expressions.

Yet for all its opulence and gaiety, an undercurrent of unease could be sensed throughout the great house, a feeling that grew steadily with each passing hour as more and more officers made their apologies and slipped away. Throughout the evening, when the orchestra fell silent for a moment, a sound from outside could clearly be heard above the hum of animated conversation. Like summer thunder, low and far away, it yet conveyed a message of infinite menace to all who heard and recognized it for what it was: the growl of distant gunfire.

Just after eleven o'clock, a cavalryman, booted and spurred, had clanked across the ballroom to bring a note to Wellington where he sat in an alcove, chatting with a group of English ladies. Wellington read the message before slipping it into his pocket and resuming his conversation, but one of the group, Lady Dalrymple-Hamilton, noticed that his manner seemed abstracted as if his thoughts were elsewhere. A few moments later he excused himself and made his way across the room to the Prince of Orange, who, after a brief conversation, nodded and left the room.

The note had contained the news that far to the southeast, at the little town of Fleurus, a French army under Marshal Grouchy had driven out the Prussian garrison. The Duke had recommended that the Prince return at once to his command, where he would shortly be needed, and in the next few minutes he dispatched after him a number of the Prince's aides, who were forced to gallop off to the front in their dancing pumps.

At the refreshment interval, as Wellington moved to take his place in the procession to the supper room across the hall, another message arrived, brought by yet another perspiring orderly, which brought the Duke's own evening to a close. He continued to chat animatedly after reading the message, but at the supper room door he disengaged himself and, taking the arm of his host, the Duke of Richmond, inquired in a whisper: "Have you a good map in the house?" It was this whisper, heard by only a few nearest to him but quickly promulgated throughout the gathering, that set everyone to speculation and discussion. What had happened, and where?

The news, which the Duke confided to no one except Richmond, was most disturbing. Prince Bernhard of Saxe-Weimar, with a small force of 4,000 infantry, mostly Dutch-Belgian conscripts, supported by eight guns, had encountered a force of 1,700 French skirmishers at Quatre Bras, the vital crossroads that linked the two Allied armies. Bernhard's farm boys had easily driven off the French, but they had then found themselves faced by a larger French force commanded by no less a personage than Marshal Ney, Napoleon's principal subordinate and celebrated as "the bravest of the brave."

The tall wheat in the fields occupied by Bernhard had hidden the weakness of his garrison from Ney's telescope, and the French force had encamped on the slope opposite

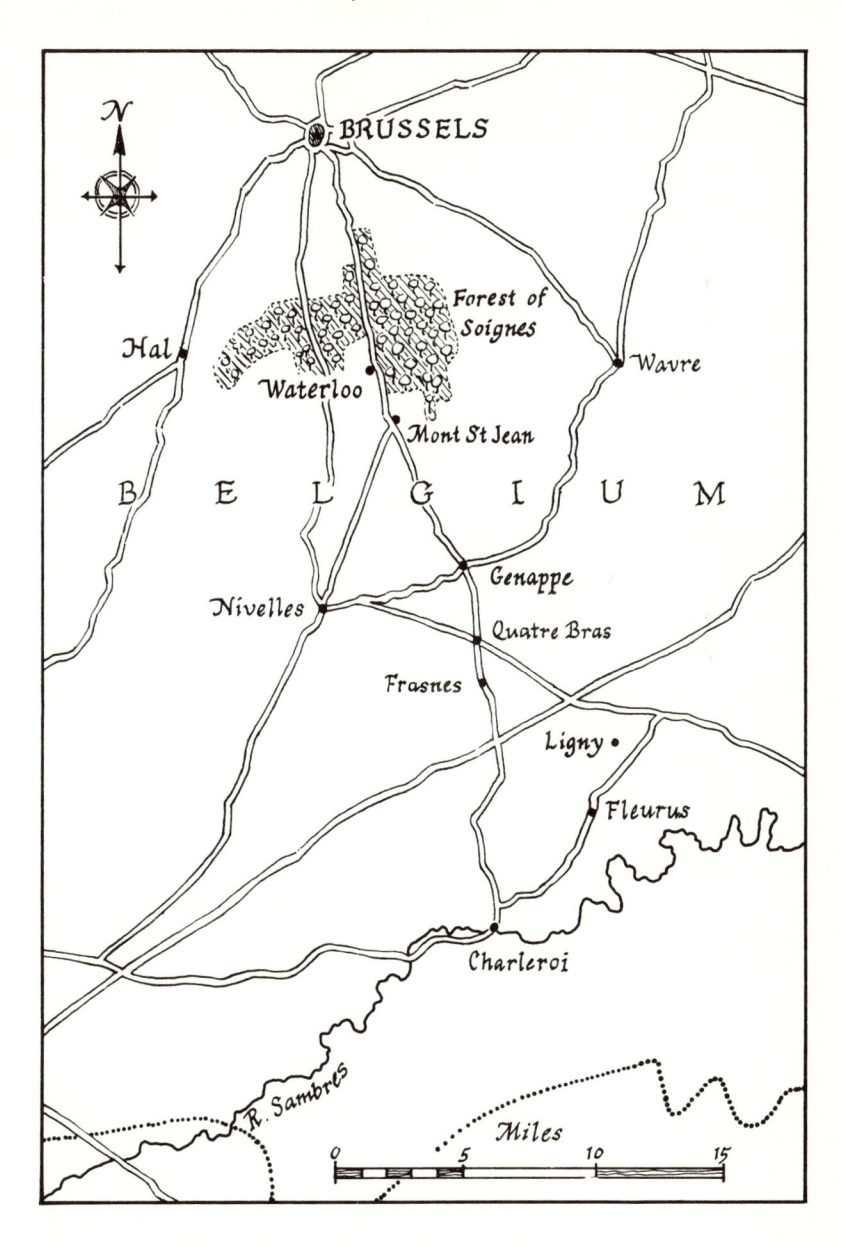

The Waterloo Campaign, June 1815

to await reinforcements. But the message showed Wellington that the French were advancing up two diverging roads, one column threatening Ligny and the other Quatre Bras. Which was the feint and which the real attack?

In the privacy of Richmond's study, Wellington pored over the map produced by his host. "We are concentrating our force at Quatre Bras," he confided, "but we shall not stop Napoleon there. If he comes on, we must fight him here," indicating with his thumbnail a position just south of the village of Waterloo.

The Duke was now all animation, and eager to be about his business. With murmured thanks to his host, who escorted him to a side door to avoid the hurly-burly at the front, he departed for his headquarters.

From her window Magdalene watched him enter his hotel and observed the flurry of activity that followed, with messengers mounting and dismounting and officers of the highest rank hurrying in and out. But her main interest was in the room behind her, where her husband still sat, scribbling orders for the stream of orderlies who clanked up and down the stairs and into their room. He had worked at that table all night long, while the sound of distant music had wafted through the open window from the Duchess's ball down the street. From time to time she had brought a fresh cup of tea to set by De Lancey's elbow, and he had looked his thanks at her before turning again to his work, but, true to her promise, in all those long hours she had spoken not a word. Great events were in train and her personal feelings must not be allowed to intrude; she was happy just to be near her husband at his moment of greatest testing and to be able to sustain him with tea and her loving presence.

It was well after four o'clock on the morning of Friday, June 16, before De Lancey was finished, the last marching orders and route instructions dispatched, the last jackbooted trooper sent off with the last message in his pouch.

As he pushed back his chair and relaxed with a yawn and a stretch, he looked over to the window seat where Magdalene still sat. The sight of her brought him back to the personal world and he was engulfed in a wave of tenderness. They rose together, moved by the same instinct, and in a moment they were in each other's arms, murmuring endearments between kisses.

A bugle call from outside the window diverted their attention. It was followed a few seconds later by another, and yet another. The buglers of the cavalry regiments billeted in the town were sounding boot and saddle! Soon half the town would be astir, for there were thousands of infantrymen billeted about who would be roused once the cavalrymen were busy with their mounts, and who would be falling in by regiment in every park and square.

It was time to make ready for their own departure. As they clung to each other, De Lancey explained the plans that had been made. Once the troops marched out, Brussels would not be a safe place for the English women staying there. Apart from the threat of French pillagers breaking into the city, the Belgian populace itself could not be trusted if the fortunes of war should go against the Allies. For safety, Magdalene and Emma should leave at daybreak for Antwerp on the coast, near enough to receive prompt news from the battlefield but handy to British ships in the harbor which could carry them to safety in England if things should go wrong. On arrival in Antwerp, Magdalene was to contact Captain Mitchell in the quartermaster department of the military depot, who would find lodgings for Emma and herself. De Lancey would send word to her immediately the battle was over, he assured her. Magdalene, too overcome for words, merely nodded her head, her face on his shoulder, and De Lancey lowered his face into her curls and held her close.

There was growing commotion in the square outside: the shouting of orders, the sound of running feet, and then the clattering of innumerable horses' hooves. In the room above, the lovers moved to the window, looking down on the animated scene below.

Within the space of minutes, the city had come alive. Lights twinkled from a thousand windows and streamed through open doorways, shouts and cries filled the air as soldiers poured into the streets, some of them with women still clinging to them or calling after them. A column of light cavalry was entering the square, a regiment of hussars in the van, the horses blowing and shying at the sudden activity. Their riders, gay in their gold-frogged jackets and striped pantaloons, their pelisses and sabretaches swinging jauntily, were still adjusting their equipment and chin-stays as they jingled past. They were followed by squadrons of lancers, pennons fluttering from the tips of their long lances, their curious flat-topped headgear, like so many scholars' mortarboards, bobbing up and down to the movement of the horses.

Out in the center of the square, Sir Thomas Picton was marshaling his division in a sort of orderly maelstrom. There was enough light now for the De Lanceys to make out the long ranks of Picton's riflemen, their uniforms a denser dark against the pavement, with the white gaiters and tall bonnets of the kilted Highlanders next to them. As the ranks lengthened and took shape, the tumult gradually diminished to a few shouted commands.

There came a silence, shocking in its abruptness. From their window the De Lanceys watched Sir Thomas pacing slowly through the ordered ranks. The stillness continued a moment following the inspection, and then, at a word of command the long lines turned and became a column, and the division moved off. The Rifle Brigade led the way, marching in silence to the tuck of a drum, swinging along easily at a steady pace, carrying their long rifles at the trail rather than in the shouldered position normal to regiments of the line. They looked a remarkably formidable lot, De

Lancey thought, looking down at their purposeful faces and steady bearing. But their somber passing was quickly eclipsed by the Highlanders in their wake, marching to the stirring strains of "Heiland Laddie" on the bagpipes and the thunder of their drums. The long column of Scottish soldiers marched for the Namur gate, their gaitered legs moving as one, their plaids and kilts and sporrans swinging in the inimitable Highland swagger, yet so steady that the De Lanceys, looking down from above, could see that the dark plumes on their bonnets hardly quivered in the still air. They were magnificent fighting men, and were obviously well aware of it; De Lancey could only wish that there were more of them.

Across the square a group of horsemen had gathered in front of the hotel headquarters where their commander-in-chief had managed to snatch a couple of hours of the deep slumber for which he was noted; Wellington had the ability to drop off to sleep instantly whatever the situation, and to awaken with all his faculties alert when roused. The officers of his staff were chatting animatedly as they sat their mounts, and De Lancey could guess that their conversation would be more of speculation than fact; few officers in the Allied army apart from himself were aware of Wellington's intentions.

The time had come for him to join them. Gazing into Magdalene's eyes, he was aware of a dreadful doubt, of a sudden, all-pervasive fear as if a chill had enveloped the room and snuffed out the light. Exhausted by the long night's toil, drained by lack of sleep of the easy confidence normal to healthy youth, he was seized by a sudden dread of what the morrow would bring.

In an agony too acute for words, the lovers embraced for the last time in the little room where they had known such happiness, and then De Lancey was clattering down the stairs to where his anxious orderly awaited with his horse, already saddled and impatient to be moving. Magdalene masked her feelings by calling after him: was there food and drink in his saddlebags, had he remembered to pack his waterproof cape? In such homely concerns there was a kind of comfort, something to keep her mind from turning to more dreadful worries, and Magdalene forced herself to watch, with pride, the obvious esteem and respect with which the assembled staff officers greeted De Lancey as he joined them at Wellington's door.

A few moments later Wellington himself appeared, greeted his waiting officers with a cheerful word, and then rode off at the head of a jingling cavalcade. De Lancey, she noticed, dropped back to near the end of the little procession, and as he rode by he turned to look upward to her window. He waved when he saw her there, and she fluttered her handkerchief and blew him a kiss. And then he was lost to sight, and suddenly the square, the room, were empty, and she was left alone.

It was full daylight when Emma bustled into the room, busy with preparations for their coming departure. Together they assembled their few belongings, Emma keeping up an excited chatter about the coming battle and the difficulties they themselves might expect to encounter on the trip to Antwerp. The music of a band outside, growing steadily louder, interrupted the flow and sent her to the window. "Oh ma'am, do come and see!" she called, and Magdalene moved to her side and looked out over her shoulder.

The square below was filled with marching troops, but the soldiers were quite unlike the brightly uniformed regiments that had gone before. These were German troops, Brunswickers mostly, and they were dressed entirely in black out of respect for the death of their ruler, killed by the French at the battle of Jena nine years before. The whole army had been put into official mourning, with black uniforms and a silver death's head grinning from their shakos, and as they filled the square with their funereal splendor they brought a stab of fear and apprehension to Magdalene's heart. Looking down from her window high above the moving blocks of black, each topped with dark plumes, she thought the column looked like a procession of gigantic hearses.

5
The Babes in the Wood

THE GORDONS LAY at their ease in the trampled wheat behind the crest of the hill, chatting in low voices as if the French, across the valley at Frasnes a mile away, might overhear. They looked relaxed and confident, De Lancey thought as he sat his horse in their midst; some were even smoking their short-stemmed clay pipes, but all had their muskets primed and loaded and ready to hand and had only to stand up to re-form the square that had so devastated the French hussars half an hour before.

Half a dozen brightly uniformed corpses marked the limit of the French foray, victims of the murderous single volley, delivered at the word of command, which was all that had been required to bring the cavalrymen to an abrupt halt and send them downhill again in confusion. One of their horses lay nearby; shot through the neck and shoulder, it had lain screaming until a Highlander had been ordered out of the square to dispatch it with a bayonet.

The encounter had been not so much an attack as a sort of tentative probe, De Lancey was sure. Ney there, across the way with some 20,000 men, had been trying to establish the size and disposition of the Allied forces hidden in the wheatfields opposite and had sent his light cavalry foward to investigate. Well, they had investigated, De

Lancey thought to himself, as he reflected with some satisfaction on the looks of amazement and horror on the cavalrymen's faces as they had suddenly found themselves confronted by a regiment of red-coated Highlanders, seemingly ten feet tall with their towering bonnets, rising out of the wheatfield with muskets already leveled.

After this brief experimental encounter, there had been a lull of sorts, and the 92nd Highlanders had taken full advantage of it to enjoy their first interval of rest since they had marched out the Namur gate in the early hours of the morning. But for De Lancey himself, after his all-night labors, there had been little rest since he had ridden out from Brussels with Wellington.

It was a chattering, glittering group that rode through the suburbs of Brussels en route to the junction of highways called Quatre Bras. The group of staff officers and aides was swollen with various distinguished gentlemen, both soldiers and civilians, anxious for a word with the commander-in-chief, all too often simply wanting to be seen in his company. There were the divisional commanders, of course, and the Earl of Uxbridge, his cavalry commander, all of whom had business with the Duke, but as the little cavalcade jingled on it was joined by General Alava, the Spanish ambassador, and by a cluster of civilian gentlemen, led by the Duke of Richmond, all anxious to hear from Wellington himself of Allied prospects in the coming battle.

It was difficult to concentrate on the business at hand in the midst of this cavalcade, and De Lancey eased his horse out of the press and fell in beside Fitzroy Somerset, an old friend and the Duke's principal aide-de-camp.

It was exactly ten o'clock in the morning when Wellington drew rein in the little village of Quatre Bras and looked about him. The young Prince of Orange was there, with his small force of Dutch and Belgians who had peppered the advancing French the evening before and were now fairly bursting with pride and confidence. Looking out from his hilltop position, however, Wellington could see little to reinforce that confidence. Across the shallow valley, no more than two miles away in the village of Frasnes, was a French force, camped in full view, that obviously outnumbered the Prince's little army by a wide margin. There might be all of 20,000 men across there, the Duke considered, studying the enemy through his pocket telescope, and more than fifty guns. It was essential to deploy the British and German regiments now en route from Brussels, twenty-one miles away, as quickly as they arrived, if any new French assault was to be held. And held it must be, for this crossroads, linking Brussels to the north with Blücher's Prussians at Ligny, six miles to the west, was the key to Allied unity and mutual support. If it should fall to the French, Napoleon would have succeeded in intervening between the two armies of his opponents, and could set about defeating them separately.

Everything seemed reasonably quiet, apart from a little popping of musketry in the valley below where the light forces of the two armies were feeling each other out. The Prince of Orange had taken up a prudent position on the crest of the hill, out of harm's way, with his troops largely screened by the standing crop of wheat which farmers thereabouts grew to a height of five feet or more to take advantage of the straw. Nothing much could be done until reinforcements started to arrive down the Brussels road, and it was essential to make contact with the Prussians to the eastward and to learn what Blücher had in mind. Accordingly, Wellington, accompanied only by De Lancey and Somerset and a pair of troopers, set off at a brisk canter down the road toward Ligny, where they arrived about one o'clock. They were met by Captain Henry Hardinge, Wellington's liaison officer with the Prussians, and were promptly shown into the country inn where Blücher had established his headquarters.

The Prussian Field Marshal, burly and bluff but genial as ever, made them welcome before leading his visitors up to the windmill of Bussy, standing on the top of the ridge behind the village. Arrived at the top, the Duke and the Field Marshal leveled their telescopes on the low hills opposite, where the French were massing their troops, while De Lancey and Gneisenau, his Prussian opposite number, surveyed the scene a respectful few paces to the rear.

A remarkable sight met the Duke's eyes; on a knoll directly opposite stood a small group of French staff officers, and in their midst was the unmistakable figure of Napoleon himself, his telescope trained upon them. For a matter of seconds, the leaders of the French, Prussian, and British forces regarded one another, before swinging their telescopes to view other features of the situation.

The Duke clearly did not like what he saw and, as his agitation increased, De Lancey swung his own telescope in the direction in which his commander-in-chief was looking. Wellington had focused on the positions his Prussian allies had taken, and as soon as he too saw them, De Lancey shared his superior's anxiety.

The Prussian troops were drawn up in solid blocks, both infantry and cavalry, in close formation on the forward slopes of the ridge, facing directly across the valley toward their French counterparts, without any attempt at cover or concealment and exposed to the direct fire of Napoleon's artillery, already massed within easy range. Turning aside with a worried look on his usually impassive face, the Duke muttered to De Lancey, "If *I* fought in such a position, I should expect to be given a most damnable mauling!"

The Duke turned back to remonstrate with Blücher, who heard him out with an air of complete unconcern. De Lancey saw fit to raise the matter with Gneisenau, who, as the Field Marshal's chief of staff, was responsible for the tactical arrangement of his troops. Gneisenau listened as De Lancey explained Wellington's views on the use of the reverse slopes for positioning troops when fighting the French, who always began their battles with a tremendous artillery bombardment. But his words had no effect whatever on the Prussian chief of staff, who simply retorted: "My men like to see whom they are fighting!" Wellington, seeing that further expostulations were useless, let the matter lie with a simple, "Well, you know your men best!" and led the way down the narrow ladder that led to the rear of the mill where their horses and escort were waiting. Before mounting, he turned and gave Blücher his hand and said, "If you are attacked, I shall come to your assistance, provided always that I am not myself under attack."

"Never fear, we shall settle his business for him," responded Blücher, with a nod and a laugh in the direction of Napoleon's threatening forces on the hill opposite.

Despite such a confident send-off, it was a grave group of horsemen who cantered off toward the Anglo-Dutch armies at Quatre Bras. The Duke rode silently, wrapped in his own thoughts. From behind them, as they left the outskirts of Ligny, came the sound of three close-grouped cannon shots, followed, after deliberate pauses, by two more sets of three shots. It was the distinctive nine-shot signal that traditionally heralded the beginning of a French onslaught, Napoleon's own hallmark. Riding a little way behind their leader, Somerset and De Lancey exchanged glances.

"They're opening the ball," Somerset commented, and shook his head in worried disapproval.

They had returned to Quatre Bras to find the crossroads much changed from the peaceful scene they had left. The French had obviously been on the move. Ney, after a dilatory start surprising in a soldier of his experience, had pushed forward a series of probing attacks. The two farms below the ridge on the eastern side of the road, held by the young troops of the Prince of Orange, had both been captured after a brief attack by French light troops, and, as Wellington arrived, a similar farm on the western side of the road also was taken. All that stood between Ney and his continued advance on Brussels was the Anglo-Dutch force on the ridge and a Dutch garrison in the Bossu Wood, a large, thick, and tangled grove of trees on the right of the Allied position, running up the hill from the valley to the top of the ridge.

But already Allied reinforcements were arriving down the road from Brussels, regiment after regiment—the Duke had arrived in the nick of time. Quickly taking over from his inexperienced but supremely unworried junior commander, the Prince of Orange, he pointed out to De Lancey where he wanted the new arrivals to be positioned before galloping off to look at the situation at the eastern end of the ridge. De Lancey stationed himself in the rear of the Gordon Highlanders, where he could keep an eye on the general situation and send the arriving regiments into the fray by the shortest routes possible. First to arrive had been the Brunswickers, magnificent in their black and silver, whom he had dispatched to reinforce the young Dutchmen in the Bossu Wood, who were threatened by a cloud of French infantry descending the slopes across the valley. Now, as he stood in the rear of the lounging Highlanders, a deep voice could be heard from the valley. "*L'Empereur récompensera celui qui s'avancera!*"

It was the famous jingle used to spur on French troops to glory, the jingle shouted by a hundred French commanders on battlefields all over Europe, and it could only come now from one man. It was Marshal Ney himself, "the bravest of the brave," going down the line in person to inspire his troops, and it could mean only one thing: a massive French attack was about to be launched on the ridge itself. Over on his left De Lancey could hear Picton's loud voice rallying his Fifth Division, and all about him the Highlanders formed up, three ranks deep, pointing a bristling array of muskets and bayonets toward the unseen enemy.

Unseen but not unheard. Below them the Gordon Highlanders could hear the shouts and singing of thousands of Frenchmen as their dense columns stamped their way up the hill, their drums thundering out the rhythm that would culminate in the furious *pas de charge.*

"*Vive l'Empereur!*" came the hoarse shout from below, as the French grenadiers began their upward climb. Moments later the same shout, louder and deeper now, rose from thousands of throats as the columns neared the crest of the ridge. A low command from their colonel, amplified by their sergeants, lowered the front rank of the Highlanders to one knee. The remaining two ranks behind were spaced so that each man had a clear field of fire over the plumed bonnets of the front rank.

The French were almost upon them now, though as yet unseen behind the tall wheat. French drums beat the rapid rhythm of an infantry charge as the voices of the sergeants and corporals urged their ranks on. Behind them a constant undertone of noise swelled—the thudding of thousands of heavy boots, the rattle and jingle of equipment and accoutrements, the growls and curses of men nerving themselves to kill or be killed.

Suddenly the French burst clear of the standing crops, a dense mass of blue-uniformed grenadiers. Their tall bearskin busbies, fierce moustaches, and stern faces gave them a fearsome aspect. On they came until, when they were still thirty yards away, men in their front rank began to loose off shots at the Highlanders, standing solid and silent before them. Most of the shots were fired only in the general direction of the British lines, before the French lowered their bayonets for the final charge across the intervening space. Down the waiting ranks of Highlanders the crisp order rang out: "Present!" A thousand muskets leveled at the advancing French. The front files of grenadiers were close upon them now, their faces contorted with the passion of the charge. Each Highlander picked out his man in the close-packed French column. At last came the long-awaited word of command from the kilted colonel in the center of the regiment: "Fire!"

The impact of a thousand lead musket balls, each the size of a songbird's egg, on the dense mass of the French column could be heard as well as seen. It stopped the charging Frenchmen in their tracks. The whole front of the massed French body disintegrated in a tangled mass of dead and dying. Yet the weight of the column behind pushed more men to the front. They stumbled over the fallen dead and wounded, firing and shouting their defiance. A second volley, crashing out at a range of no more than thirty feet, sent the whole mass tumbling back in a tangle of shoving, cursing men, their retreat mercifully hidden by clouds of smoke and dust from the remorseless British muskets. At a word from their colonel, the Gordons once again stood at ease, grinning and boasting now as they looked to their locks and loading.

For De Lancey, it was Spain all over again. The reverse slope behind the crest of the ridge had proved itself time and time again, on a dozen Peninsular battlefields, sparing troops there from the direct cannonade and sharpshooter fire that were always the opening moves of a Napoleonic assault. Now, as before, the British muskets, fired on the word of command by disciplined troops deployed in line, had repulsed the dense-packed French infantry column, despite all its fervor and élan.

Satisfied that all was well on this section of the front, De Lancey turned his attention to the dusty road behind, where British regiments, cavalry now as well as infantry, were arriving to reinforce Wellington's tenuous position. The cavalry were sent eastward, where the Duke was already mounting counterattacks on the captured farms in front of the ridge. He fed the red-coated line regiments into the front line as they arrived, giving him for the first time something like numerical parity with Ney's assault forces.

But both the Duke and his quartermaster general were to receive a rude shock at the western end of the British line, where a heavy French attack was delivered on the Bossu Wood, which was held by two young Dutch regiments with a stiffening of Brunswick infantry. Frightened by the fearsome aspect of the advancing French columns and demoralized by the sharpshooters and light troops infiltrating the woods all about them, the raw Dutch levies cracked, retreated deeper into the woods, and finally took to their heels in panic before the enemy. Their headlong flight became a rout that carried the uncertain Brunswickers with them; a few minutes after the first French attack a mass of Dutch and German soldiers poured from the woods, heading for the paved road that led back to Brussels and safety.

Ney saw their flight from the heights opposite, and was quick to seize his opportunity. Soon squadrons of French light cavalry, hussars and lancers, were hacking and spitting the hapless fugitives as they ran. The throng of struggling men, pursuers and pursued, encountered a column of supply wagons and camp followers making their way out from Brussels. In seconds the highway was strewn with abandoned carts as an avalanche of desperate men rushed headlong back to Brussels, carrying all before them. And as they went, the fugitives spread wild tales of French victory and Allied disaster.

Indeed, something very near disaster almost overtook the Allies. The young Duke of Brunswick, as he tried to rally his broken troops, was hit in the stomach by a musket ball and was carried from the field mortally wounded. Meanwhile, the Duke of Wellington, riding across the ridge with Fitzroy Somerset to see for himself how things stood at the Bossu Wood, was nearly cut off by a troop of French hussars and the pair had to ride for their lives, with the French close behind. Reaching a hedge behind which the Gordon Highlanders were formed up, the Duke called in his loud, nasal voice, "Ninety-second—*lie down!*" With Somerset following close behind, he put Copenhagen, his magnificent chestnut horse, to the jump and cleared both ditch and the front rank of the Highlanders, whose sharp volley into the pursuing hussars soon drove the Frenchmen back down the hill.

The Duke and young Somerset found themselves in the center of a grinning group of Scotsmen, and De Lancey congratulated his commander-in-chief on his horsemanship with a smile that won an answering laugh from the Duke. "That," said Wellington, "was a damned near-run thing!"

The advantage won by the French cavalry soon abated with the arrival of the main body of British horse, which had been delayed in making its way from Brussels. Yet the situation in the wood itself was still unclear and, after a brief discussion with Wellington, De Lancey, with a handful of troopers, rode over to the upper portions of the forest to see for himself how matters stood. Since the approaches were clear and no shots were fired at them, the little group rode a short distance into the nearest part of the wood, which here was relatively open, comprising a series of glades. Suddenly De Lancey's horse shied and plunged sideways with such violence that he was nearly unseated. As he fought to regain control of his badly frightened mount, he caught sight of a dark shape just above his head. At his exclamation, the little group drew rein alongside, and all looked up at the lower branches of the tree overhead.

The body of a boy, dressed in the distinctive bright uniform of a Nassau infantry regiment, hung upside down, caught by the waist in a fork of the tree. He had been a drummer, for though he no longer carried his drum, the slings by which it was normally carried hung down from his side. He had been shot twice through the upper part of his body, and a trickle of drying blood ran down from his open mouth. His staring eyes were bright blue, his short-cropped hair the color of straw. He could not have been more than ten years old. In the branches a little way above, another youngster, dressed in identical uniform and still wearing the same drum slings over his shoulder, huddled motionless with his knees drawn up to his chin. He, too, was blond and hatless. His long golden eyelashes were lowered and his expression was as peaceful and serene as if he had simply fallen asleep. Only the two wounds, through the back and the shoulder, showed where he had been shot as he sat, helpless and unarmed, leaving his face as pink and unblemished as any peach, his martial dress violently at odds with his childish features.

The little party of horsemen looked on in a grim silence, broken only by the oath of a trooper in the rear. No explanation was needed as to what had happened; it was all too clear. When their regiment had broken under the French attack, the two boys had abandoned their drums in order to make their escape. They would have been shouldered aside by their bigger, stronger comrades in the mad panic of retreat and, at the last, with the French close behind them, they had climbed a tree to escape. There the French *voltigeurs* had found them and there, for sport, with their marksmen's rifles, they had picked them off in the tree like a brace of sitting birds.

For the French light troops, calloused by years of foraging, looting, and rapine across the face of Europe, it had been a moment's sport, nothing more, but for De Lancey and the men about him it was a violation of the oldest rule of warfare between civilized states: women, children, and civilians were exempt from wanton killing. Certainly, even in the brutal fighting in Spain, neither French nor British had slaughtered drummer boys, cart drivers, or camp followers.

The shocked reverie was ended abruptly by a musket shot, fired from the thickets ahead. As De Lancey turned his horse about, there were more shots. A ball slammed into a tree just above him. Grim-faced, the group rode back out of the woods into the shelter of a nearby wheatfield, and thence along the ridge to the crossroads.

With Bossu Wood in the hands of the French, the whole of the western sector of the Allied line was in danger, and quick action was essential. If no reinforcements were in sight coming from Brussels, troops would have to be sent from some other sector to stabilize the situation. But as De Lancey and his little party drew rein at the crossroads, help arrived in the very nick of time. A regiment of the Guards marched up after a late start from Brussels. De Lancey had originally planned to send this regiment to form Wellington's reserve at the center of the Allied position, but their appearance at a moment of crisis seemed too good an opportunity to miss. Yet he hesitated to commit the Guards, arguably the finest line-of-battle troops in the world, to the catch-as-catch-can sort of fighting involved in clearing thick woods, a job much better done by light troops accustomed to taking cover. A rifle regiment was available a mile to the east; it would take some time to get a message to them, and even more time before they could arrive, but they could be counted on to winkle the French out of the thickets with the minimum of loss. This, of course, meant a minimum loss to *both* sides— light troops operated by driving the enemy from their positions, not by annihilating them. The Guards, on the other hand, could be counted on to inflict the maximum punishment on their opponents. Suddenly De Lancey knew that it was punishment that was called for in Bossu Wood.

Let those barbarians who had killed unarmed boys for sport see what they could do against a regiment of British footguards. Without hesitation he scribbled the orders that would clear the woods completely, and watched the trooper gallop off with the message to the oncoming troops before turning back to see how matters were progressing in the sector immediately in front.

The Gordons were now obviously heavily engaged—the sound of their rolling volleys came as a regular pattern of explosive noise, and the smoke of their musketry covered the whole front in acrid clouds that dimmed the sun. It was horsemen that Ney was now hurling at them, columns of heavy cavalry riding stirrup to stirrup up the long slopes and through the trampled fields of wheat. A wave of horsemen, seeming enormous on their great black horses, broke through the dense smoke as De Lancey watched, and thundered down upon the waiting Highlanders. A crashing volley brought many of them down and broke the momentum of the charge, but their leader, a scowl visible under his great cuirassier's helmet, spurred his mount forward, waving his saber high to encourage his wavering troopers to press home their charge.

A second volley crashed out and, when the smoke had cleared, the whole front of the enemy column had been swept away. The gallant leader, his horse shot dead, lay on the ground, but he sprang up in a moment. His helmet had been knocked from his head and, with a shock, De Lancey recognized him, more because of his stiff gray hair than his features. It was General Kellermann, a famous cavalry leader and a favorite of Napoleon himself, whom De Lancey had met in Paris shortly after Bonaparte's banishment to Elba. He cut a grotesque figure now, his bandy legs in their enormous thigh boots seeming at odds with his thick-set, burly figure encased in its heavy cuirass, but for all that, he showed why he had earned a reputation for energy and enterprise second to none.

Scrambling for his life like some two-legged crab, he thrust himself between two horses of his retreating troopers, grasped the bridles of each near the bits, and was borne from the field between the two frightened animals, his feet touching the ground in a series of giant steps.

For more than an hour the pattern of fighting continued. To his left, De Lancey could see that the Allied line was being worn desperately thin by the constant pressure of a savage, slashing attack. Sensing his advantage, Ney exerted yet more pressure and was rewarded when a surge of horsemen broke through the ranks of exhausted infantrymen and galloped on to take possession of the vital crossroads, the key to the Allied position and the object of the whole French effort. But the good fortune that had attended the Duke all day came to his aid again—another late arrival of British cavalry appeared on the scene just in time to dash the French from the road junction and drive them back in disorder to their own lines. It was the crisis and climax of the battle. After his repulse Ney drew back to his lines below the village of Frasnes, across the valley.

At half past six the bugles blew all down the long Allied line, sounding the advance. As the cheering troops poured down from their ridge-top positions where they had endured such a battering all day long, the sullen French formations retreated to the heights opposite, leaving isolated garrisons in the little farmhouses, Piraumont and Gemioncourt, which commanded the road across the valley. They were carried at the bayonet by two regiments of British infantry, but Wellington restrained the pursuit once Quatre Bras was again in his hands, and resumed his stand on the hamlet's hilltop. As the evening began to draw in, the firing gradually ceased, and the batteries on both sides of the valley fell silent. An enormous pall of smoke hung over the Bossu Wood, and hundreds of birds wheeled silently over the ravaged groves, but even there the sounds of conflict died away with the fading light.

At the end of a long day's fighting, which had cost both sides something like 5,000 casualties each, matters stood just as they had at the beginning. Wellington was still firmly astride the vital crossroads and the French were still on the slopes opposite. D'Erlon's corps of 20,000 men, which could have made a decisive contribution on either field, had spent the day marching and countermarching between Napoleon's battle at Ligny and Ney's at Quatre Bras, victims of Napoleon's indecision.

As De Lancey sat his horse, watching the last of the French cavalry trotting back down the valley, he was approached by a dusty messenger on foot, sent to report that the Guards now held Bossu Wood.

"Is the whole wood now clear of the French?" De Lancey asked.

"Ah, there's plenty of Frenchmen still there, right enough," replied the young ensign, "but they're all dead. Our fellows saw the two drummer boys, and they were giving no quarter!"

"My dearest Magdalene," De Lancey scribbled, as he dashed off a note, using his sabretache as a desk, "we have given the French a thrashing at a place called Quatre Bras. I am in the best of health." And then, because he was young and in love, he filled the rest of the page with endearments before sealing it and handing the envelope to the waiting messenger to be galloped to Brussels and Antwerp with the official dispatches.

6

The King of Spain

IT STOOD ON THE MAIN street of the little town of Genappe, three miles north of Quatre Bras on the Brussels road—a rambling, plaster-fronted country inn, with its name painted large across its façade: Le Roi d'Espagne. Here, at nine o'clock on the evening of the battle, Wellington and his staff clattered into the cobbled courtyard, handing over their horses to the inn's hostler and his helpers before seeing what food and drink the place could offer them. They were all in high spirits; Ney had been frustrated in his attempt to march on Brussels, and they were confident that Blücher's Prussians had been equally successful in turning back Napoleon at Ligny. They were also aware of the desperation of the French position. Napoleon must win a crushing victory, and win it soon, or he must lose all. Time was on the Allied side—Napoleon would never be so strong as he was at present, whereas the true strength of the Allies had only begun to be mobilized. Quatre Bras had been a rebuff for the French; a similar rebuff at Ligny must finish any ambitions Bonaparte might have of returning as Emperor of France.

The Duke was relaxed as he sat down to dinner with his staff. At any time now he expected to hear from Marshal Blücher, since the guns had fallen silent at Ligny at about the same time as the battle at Quatre Bras had ended. But as time passed without word of the Prussians, the atmosphere at the Duke's table grew concerned, then anxious. By the time De Lancey, exhausted by two hard days without sleep, had eaten a quick supper and excused himself, a certain restlessness was evident in the Duke's manner. De Lancey was glad to be able to stretch out in an upstairs bedroom, shared with three other officers, and plunge instantly into a deep, dreamless sleep. He was awakened a few hours later by an orderly shaking his shoulder and whispering to him in the darkened room that Wellington was up and wished to see him.

Pulling on his coat and boots and picking his way past the sleeping figures of his fellow officers on the floor, De Lancey crossed the hall and tapped on the door of the Duke's room. Wellington was already dressed, and within a few moments they were joined by Somerset. Down in the stableyard the horses were ready, saddled and waiting, and the trio set out at a gallop for Quatre Bras. It was just past three o'clock on the morning of Saturday, June 17, but the five hours of unbroken sleep had made a new man of De Lancey, and he was eager to address himself to the problems of a new day. The Duke was in no mood for conversation, so the three galloped through the night in silence.

Apart from sentries and a quartet of staff officers, the crossroads were deserted as the trio drew rein. All about them were the muffled figures of thousands of men, bivouacking under every available bit of shelter or in the standing crops on each side of the road. Many were huddled about fires. A hasty interchange with a duty officer who presented himself when the commander-in-chief was recognized soon established that the situation at the crossroads was unchanged, but that there had been disturbing reports of French light cavalry patrols encountered along the road to the east, to Ligny, which should still have been firmly held by Prussian cavalry.

The moment he heard this news, Wellington summoned Colonel Alexander Gordon, the best horseman on his staff, and sent him off toward Ligny to find out what had happened. The Duke was obviously in a fever of impatience; after Gordon had ridden off on his all-important mission, he dismounted, handed Copenhagen over to the attentions of an orderly, and paced briskly up and down on the pavement, where he was joined by Somerset and De Lancey. The early-morning air bit cruelly, and the three stamped their feet and blew on their ungloved hands in vain efforts to keep warm.

Near the crossroads, a rough, three-sided herdsman's shelter, made of branches and thatched with sod, drew the Duke's eye, and he stopped before it.

"Ninety-second, I will be obliged to you for a little fire," he called to a group of Highlanders gathered around their campfire, and the soldiers, basking in their famous commander's regard, were quick to respond. In moments a bright fire was warming the walls of the ramshackle shelter, and the Highlanders were rewarded with the compliments and thanks of their grateful Duke, who had now spread out his maps and established himself with his staff at this impromptu headquarters. Somerset fetched a pot of tea, and with the aid of brandy from their pocket flasks the huddled officers managed to keep the early-morning chill and damp at bay. Yet the minutes of waiting dragged on. There was little they could do until word arrived from Blücher and his Prussians.

It arrived at last, at half past seven, when Gordon clattered to a halt in front of the hut and swung himself down from a lathered, exhausted horse. It was the worst sort of news, yet Wellington's face was as impassive as ever as Gordon whispered it in his ear. The Duke turned to his staff and to the divisional commanders who had ridden in to join his vigil.

"Old Blücher has had a damned good licking and gone

back to Wavre, eighteen miles. As he has gone back, we must go too."

It was as simple as that. The British and Dutch, despite their victory the day before, must give up the Quatre Bras position they had so tenaciously defended and retire back towards Brussels if they were to maintain their unbroken line of defense. The maintenance of a common front was more important than the position of that front. All the same, it involved a retreat, and no soldier, least of all a British soldier, liked retreating, especially after what he considered to be a victorious battle.

There would be grumbling from every foot-slogging infantry private, not to mention the officers, De Lancey reflected as he contemplated the enormous task of sending orders to each unit in the Allied army. These were the orders that would form a new battle line on the high ground near the village of Waterloo, in the area already selected by Wellington as the most advantageous place to oppose a French attack. For half an hour the Duke and De Lancey pored over their lists of men and regiments, determining which should go where, and then Wellington left his quartermaster general to his paperwork. The orders were soon streaming out via a line of booted and spurred orderlies, whose horses champed restlessly at their bits as they waited to be off. The commander-in-chief had a short rest, but for De Lancey there was a two-hour period of the most intense and concentrated activity. In those two crowded hours he had to work out the timetables and routes for thousands of men and tons of matériel to take along roads already congested, through villages of doubtful loyalty, to arrive at a distant site in good order and ready to give battle to a redoubtable enemy. It was the most testing time he had yet experienced.

But by ten o'clock it was finished. The last order had been sent on its way to the last unit and De Lancey was free to rejoin the Duke where he stood, with his staff about him, at the side of the road on which a British line regiment was already forming up in column of route. A cup of tea, fresh from the fire, almost too hot to hold in its tin cup, drove the last of the morning chill from his young bones, and the prospect of a day of intense activity sent his spirits soaring.

His work was far from over. No sooner had the Duke's eye fallen on him than he called De Lancey to his side and, with a hand on his shoulder and his mouth close to De Lancey's ear, gave his young aide a challenging mission. De Lancey was to ride ahead and select a field of battle, somewhere in the area the Duke had already discussed, among the ridges and open ground south of the Forest of Soignes and the village of Waterloo. He was to choose the sort of site that offered the characteristic features of a Wellingtonian position, and the Duke mentioned a ridge he had already investigated, with its reverse slopes and good lateral communication, as a first suggestion. Once he had chosen the field, De Lancey was to mark out the areas to be occupied by different units, together with a position for the Duke's headquarters. In short, the Duke was commissioning his young American quartermaster general to choose the site on which the fate of the Allied armies was to be decided, and was doing so with every confidence. De Lancey rode off well aware of the enormous responsibility entrusted to him.

Genappe, the little town immediately to Wellington's rear, was De Lancey's first concern. Conscious of the threat its narrow streets posed to the movement of a retreating army, De Lancey had already sent his deputy, Colonel Basil Jackson, ahead to clear away all debris from its congested main street and to widen it, where possible, to accommodate the great press of traffic to be expected. Galloping into the town, De Lancey was pleased to find the work well in hand, the road clear of local traffic and projecting walls knocked down at the narrowest points.

Already a steady stream of carts laden with Allied wounded was making its way through the town. Although it would obviously be jammed when the retreating regiments of horse and foot arrived, everything possible had been done to keep the route clear, and De Lancey congratulated Jackson when he found him at the northern limits of the town, supervising the removal of piles of rubble from a demolished building.

He glanced hungrily at the King of Spain as he rode past, where a surly waiter regarded him stonily from the open coffee-room door, but he had no time to spare for a meal and he rode on without regret, although his empty stomach rumbled in protest. He pulled a sausage and a chunk of bread from his saddlebag and wolfed them down as he trotted along the road toward Waterloo, the road that thousands of men were now following.

Behind him, the retreat had begun at ten o'clock. The light troops of the Rifle Brigade, the finest marchers in the army, led the way, followed immediately by one of the regiments of Foot Guards. Wellington had stood by the side of the road to watch them pass, the men swinging along in good heart, but grousing cheerfully and audibly. One of the more venturesome even called out to their commander-in-chief, "Is this the right road to Paris?"

Some of the other units were less cheerful about abandoning a position they had so successfully defended. The Highlanders were dour and silent as they trudged back along the road toward Brussels. Picton, their commander, was particularly sour-faced and surly, as he was nursing two broken ribs from his encounter with the French cavalry the previous afternoon. But the philosophic resignation of the infantry soldier toward the vagaries of fate and the higher command was proof against even this latest turn of events, and the Duke was reassured by the obvious high spirits and morale of the British infantry regiments that made up the heart of his polyglot army.

Last to march were the Allied cavalry. The heavy brigade moved first, with the light regiments—hussars mostly, with a stiffening of Life Guards—and the mounted batteries of the Horse Artillery providing a rearguard screen. As these last clattered onto the crossroads, Wellington swung himself into the saddle and rode to the ridge overlooking Frasnes and the French lines. All seemed strangely silent; perhaps Ney, too, was in retreat.

In any event, the Duke was only too happy to be able to move off without any interference from a curiously somnolent enemy. The long line of carts carrying British and Dutch and German wounded was already strung out from Quatre Bras to Genappe, but this most vulnerable of targets would soon be beyond the logjam of Genappe and safe from any French pursuit.

At two o'clock in the afternoon the last Allied regiment marched away up the Brussels road, and Wellington turned to Lord Uxbridge, who commanded the rearguard, as the two sat overlooking the French lines. "Well, Uxbridge, no use waiting. The sooner you get away the better. No time to be lost." He wheeled Copenhagen about, but before he could move away, a sudden ejaculation from Uxbridge caused him to turn and follow the other's pointing finger. "Lancers, my lord!" It was an awesome, a stupendous, sight; a moment that all who witnessed it would remember, with wonder, all their lives.

A dense column of cavalry, their lance points twinkling in the thin sunlight, was pouring down the Frasnes slopes, sending a vast cloud of white dust billowing high above the trees that had hidden them. An unearthly light cast deep shadows as a tremendous thundercloud, black and pendulous, swallowed up the pale sunlight. A chill wind blew down the valley, and a dark shadow spread over the British rearguard positions as the ink-black thundercloud drew closer, low and ominous. For an instant, the figure of a solitary horseman stood illuminated by a shaft of sunlight against the brilliant fields across the valley, a figure instantly recognized by the British officers as Napoleon himself, just arrived from Ligny. There was a shattering detonation and a sheet of flame as the British guns opened fire, to be followed a second later by a thunderclap like the end of the world as the huge stormcloud burst apart with a flash and a roar. The rain fell in torrents, with a din that drowned out all other sound; the world seemed shrouded in a curtain of falling water wherein retreating British and advancing French—men, horses, and guns— were intermixed in a deadly ballet of shadows.

But the storm, for all its intensity, was brief and local. When Wellington and his staff trotted into Genappe in mid-afternoon, the warm sun shone down on streets still crowded with retreating regiments, horse and foot, and the last straggling carts, laden with wounded and supplies. Colonel Jackson labored mightily in the narrowest places to keep traffic moving, using the flat of his sword and the oaths and imprecations of three languages to sort out the worst tangles.

In such a situation it seemed best to the Duke to dine early at the King of Spain inn, to allow time for the last units to get clear of the town and for his rearguard to catch up. Accordingly, he and his staff sat down to enjoy whatever the inn could offer in its crowded coffee room.

It was a cheerful meal, the conversation all the more animated because of the circumstances, but the Duke was horrified to hear, during a lull in the table talk, an officer call out to a friend across the room: "Old Blücher is marching to join us at Waterloo!"

This, of course, was vital and secret information, known only to Colonel Gordon, who had brought it from Ligny, and to the Duke and his closest staff. It was monstrous that it should be bandied about in a public place, and the Duke growled a rebuke to the now-mortified speaker. There were waiters in the room and other civilians whose loyalty could not be counted upon, and a shocked silence descended upon the gathering, to be dispelled only gradually as normal conversation was resumed. An hour later, when the little group of officers, refreshed by their rest and restored by a pleasant meal, swung again into their saddles, the incident had been forgotten.

By late afternoon they were approaching their destination, and at about the same time a party of French cavalry officers, following in the wake of their advanced screen, drew rein in front of the King of Spain. They were talking excitedly; some of them had been caught up in brisk fighting as their leading troopers had come up with the rear rank of the retreating British rearguard, but at the outer limits of the town a charge by a company of the Life Guards had driven back the leading files, and the pursuit had lost much of its momentum when the French colonel commanding the lancers had been killed in a hand-to-hand clash with the dashing Captain Edward Kelly of the Life Guards.

They filled the coffee room of the old inn with their animated conversation, sitting at ease with their spurred and booted feet asprawl at the tables where, only two hours before, Wellington and his staff had likewise taken their ease. Their senior officer, a short, swarthy, dark-eyed man in a uniform gorgeous with gold lace, was treated with deference by his younger companions, and it was this older man whom one of the waiters now sought out. The French officer, impatient at the interruption, swung round to hear what the waiter—the same surly servant who had stared stonily after the passing De Lancey, and who had been waiting at the Duke's table a couple of hours before—had to say. But the whispered message cleared all signs of irritation from the French officer's face, and he turned back to face his puzzled companions.

"Wellington has been here just before us," he explained.

"This man waited on him, and he says Blücher and the Prussians are marching to join the British at Waterloo!"

It was momentous news. It meant that Napoleon, who had thought that the Prussians were in full retreat home to Prussia, and who had now joined his army to that of Ney in the hope of overwhelming Wellington's troops as he had Blücher's, might yet have to face a combined British-Prussian army. Napoleon had delayed half a day at Ligny before marching to join Ney at Frasnes, and that delay might now cost him dearly. Certainly he must hasten to bring Wellington to battle before Blücher could intervene.

But, momentous as his information was, the waiter was unaware of a circumstance even more singular. For, all unknown to him, the French officer he was addressing was none other than Jérôme Bonaparte, King of Westphalia and brother both to the Emperor and to Joseph, who called himself still by the title painted on the front of the inn: "Le Roi d'Espagne," the King of Spain.

7

Waterloo

STANDING ON THE RIDGE looking down into the shallow valley, De Lancey regarded the features of the place with enormous satisfaction; this, surely, was the ideal site on which to fight the battle his commander-in-chief had in mind. This ridge, and the woods, fields, and roads that surrounded it, offered all the advantages of terrain that he had been hoping to find, and he must now set about positioning the Allied troops to make full use of every feature.

Although he had the best eye for country of any officer on Wellington's staff (which was why he, a young, relatively junior, American-born officer, had been chosen to select the field of battle), he had happened upon this place quite by accident. With three junior officers and a company of troopers, he had gone first to the particular site selected and reconnoitered long before by Wellington himself. It had had the qualities the Duke considered essential—the reverse slopes, the lateral communications, the good field of fire—but as he rode along it De Lancey had been disturbed by its size. Wellington had been considering it for occupation by a combined Anglo-Prussian army, much larger than his present shrunken force, which would simply be swallowed up by these distances, De Lancey could see. This smaller army would have to be extended into long, attenuated lines, much too fragile to stand up to sustained attack, simply to fill the open space on the ridgetop. If it were to be concentrated into more durable formations it would leave both flanks open to attack, and he well knew the ability of the ferocious French cavalry to exploit such an opportunity, given such room to maneuver. This great expanse of open field along the ridgetop would be a death trap for the Duke's army, and De Lancey had been forced to search somewhere else for a suitable site.

But in looking about him from his hilltop vantage point, his eye had fallen on another low ridge immediately to the north, across the valley in the direction of Brussels. Even from a distance some of its features could be appreciated: open ground overlooking the valley and offering a good field of fire, and a much more compact position than the first location. With high hopes, he had cantered across at the head of his little troop, to find everything he could possibly have wished for.

To begin with, this position dominated the main north-south road, the all-important route to Brussels, lying astride the road as it breasted the ridge. A minor east-west road, leading to Wavre, provided the good lateral communications needed to shift troops from one flank to the other, and the little village of Waterloo in the rear provided an ideal site for a headquarters. The enemy, of course, would be given the use of the site originally noticed by Wellington, but in reverse—the low valley between would afford an excellent field of fire for the Allied artillery, as it was dominated for its full length by the heights of the Allied front. All in all a fine position, with the Forest of Soignes covering the rear and each flank, and the Brussels road offering an easy route for reinforcements or withdrawal. And there was another feature that might be used to advantage, De Lancey considered, looking over the ground with a meditative eye. To the right of the Allied

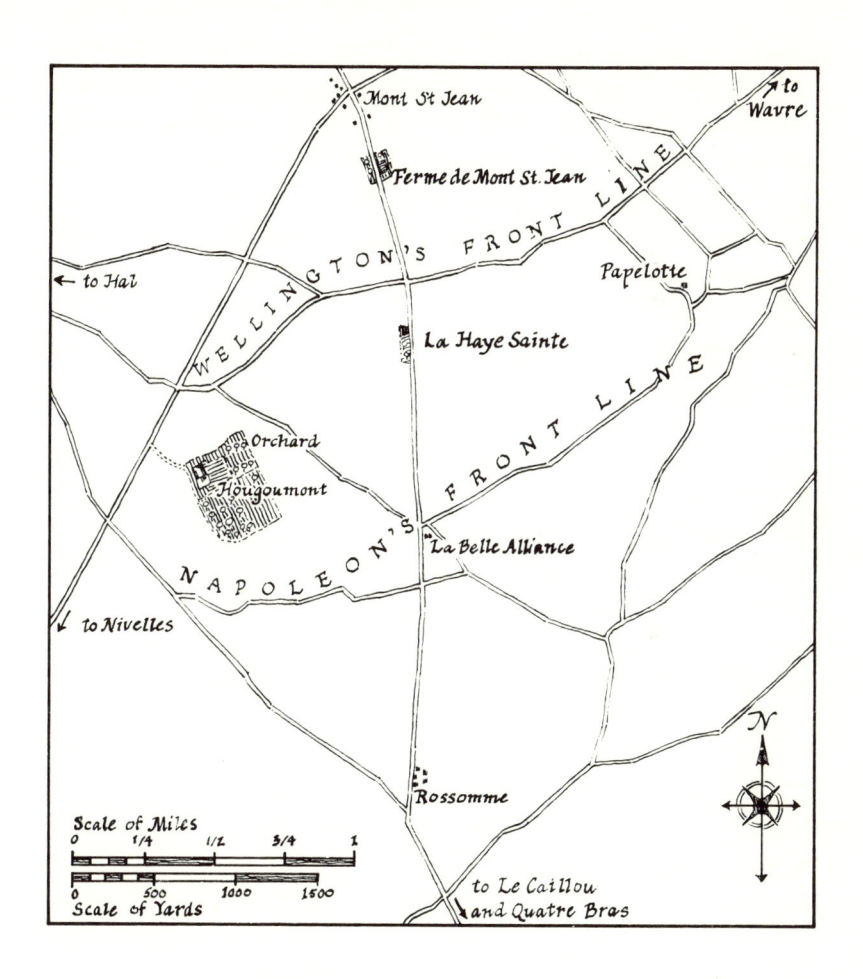

The Battlefield of Waterloo, June 18, 1815

front, in the valley below, there was a walled farmhouse, Hougoumont, and in the center of the position, right next to the Brussels road itself, was another farmhouse, called La Haye Sainte. With their high sides, numerous outbuildings, and surrounding walls, each of these farms would form a formidable outpost if properly garrisoned. Hougoumont in particular, with its enclosed orchard and rectangular shape, would be a very strong position indeed. Filled with troops and well supplied, these two outlying strongpoints would be very difficult for any enemy to overthrow and would tend to disrupt even the strongest attacks attempting to bypass them. They were the deciding factor, De Lancey thought; this was the place to challenge Napoleon and his veteran army, and he quickly set about the business of marking it out.

Armed with stakes, chalk, and crayons and directed by their officers, his troopers soon had the ridgetop battle line clearly set out, with the position marked where each unit was to place itself. At two o'clock that afternoon, when the first Allied unit appeared, marching up the Brussels road, everything was ready for them. Later in the day, when the Duke swung off his horse at the little inn directly across from the village chapel in Waterloo and walked into what now was his headquarters, he congratulated De Lancey on his choice of field. He admitted that he had been surprised to find his original choice empty, but he could appreciate this new and stronger position. With De Lancey and a group of staff officers, including the Earl of Uxbridge (who had just arrived with the last of the rearguard), he remounted half an hour later and trotted down the road past the hamlet and farmhouse of Mont St. Jean to a little knoll that overlooked the whole extent of the valley.

All along the ridge British, Dutch, Belgian, and German regiments were taking up their positions. The men, weary after a long day's march, piled their muskets, unrolled their blankets, and prepared to bivouac in the open as best they could. Fires were lit, cooking pots produced, and groups of soldiers, many already smoking their pipes, made themselves as comfortable as possible. Infantry regiments, each a block of color in their distinctive uniforms, were strung out along the ridge, while behind them, their horses already tethered in orderly lines to bayonets driven into the ground, the cavalry were facing up to the double task of feeding and making comfortable both men and mounts.

Across the valley, on the shallow ridge forming the reverse of the position once favored by Wellington, the French were now arriving, a confused mass of various colors and flashing steel, blurred by distance and the failing light. As dusk drew in they could be seen pouring down the road from Quatre Bras and taking up their positions along the crest of the hill; soon their campfires were twinkling like so many fireflies among the dark fields. De Lancey, who knew the ground better than anyone, told the Duke that Napoleon would likely choose a little country inn called La Belle Alliance, located on the hill beside the Brussels road, for his headquarters, although he might prefer to spend the night at the village of Le Caillou further to the rear, because of its more suitable accommodation for the housing of his large staff. Wellington regarded the French movements with an impassive face before shutting his telescope with a snap and cantering back to Waterloo for the night with most of his staff, leaving De Lancey alone to survey the arrival of the last British troops.

The two armies that were to contest this field were now in place and, as he rode slowly along the Allied line, De Lancey could not help reflecting on the curious contrast between the two forces. Here, all about him, were regiments from Belgium, Holland, and various small principalities which were now ostensibly anti-Napoleon, but which had all once been part of his empire. Many of these

Belgians, for instance, had fought for the French in previous campaigns and had friends and even relatives serving in French units on the other side of the valley. All conscripts, they could hardly be expected to view the coming battle with much enthusiasm, having arrived at this situation merely through some politician's change of heart. The Dutch units were made up of mere youngsters, raw conscripts taking part in their first campaign; they could hardly be counted on to stand up to too much punishment in tomorrow's battle. Still, some of them had made a creditable showing in their blooding at Quatre Bras, and they seemed animated enough now as they prepared to spend a night in the open, which was more than could be said of some of the Belgians. As he rode through their lines, De Lancey was aware of a generally surly attitude, and there were some black looks directed at him, even from some of the officers, probably those who had served under the Emperor before and were in no mood to oppose him now. These were the regiments that would seize the first opportunity to desert or defect the moment they could safely do so, and De Lancey was happy to pass on to where he had positioned a British encampment.

The difference in attitude was striking. De Lancey found himself in the midst of a noisy bustle, its cheerfulness evident even despite the perpetual grousing so typical of the British soldier in the field—the constant complaining about the food, the weather, and the vagaries of command. Hearing the rough banter, for the men were in good heart despite a trying day's marching and the prospect of yet another night of lying out in the open, De Lancey felt both his spirits and his confidence rise. All about him were men who could be counted on to do the job, come what might, and he chatted happily with a group of their officers before passing on to the cavalry lines.

Here all was in order, as might be expected of such old campaigners. British cavalry, especially such units as the

Life Guards and the Blues, were the élite of the British army, and their magnificent horses, picketed in orderly lines, were already being fed and tended by their assiduous troopers. But although they might rank at the top of the army's pecking order, the true strength of the Duke's force lay in the British infantry, the red-coated line regiments, and it was on them that the outcome of tomorrow's battle chiefly depended. And although many of the individual soldiers and even some entire regiments were raw and untested in action, De Lancey knew they could be counted upon. He had fought with them, or with men and regiments just like them, for all his adult life, and knew what they were capable of. They were not so nimble as the French, nor so expert at foraging in the field or in exploiting an opportunity to attack, but their disciplined endurance was legendary and their musketry the marvel of Europe.

Walking his horse slowly through their bivouac, De Lancey was in a reflective mood. This Allied force was a patchwork affair, cobbled together from whatever units were available to the politicians of a new and shaky alliance. Over there, across the valley, was a veteran, homogeneous army, the most formidable in the world, victors of a hundred battles, who had marched into every capital in Europe. Like all British soldiers, De Lancey had learned to respect his French counterpart, and to admire some of his abilities, but he was equally well aware of the peculiarities that set the French army apart from others in the field. Bonaparte's insistence that the army must "live off the land," sustaining itself on whatever food was available in the vicinity of where it found itself, had turned its men into the most accomplished thieves and pillagers since Attila; an army that lived by robbery, rape, and torture, and left desolation behind it. The French army lived and died for glory, not just for France but more particularly for their Emperor. Yet that same Emperor, for all his dynamic genius, thought nothing of sacrificing those same adoring soldiers whenever expedient. Perhaps never before in history, De Lancey reflected, had the ambitions of one man brought so much death and misery to so many people in so many countries.

He had abandoned one army in Egypt and an even larger one in Russia, and his ruthlessness when his personal schemes were involved was legendary. When he had found a surrendered Mameluke army in Egypt too difficult to feed, he had resolved the problem by ordering it put to death. When an officer remonstrated, pointing out that to shoot so many thousands of men would consume much valuable powder and scarce shot, Bonaparte had merely altered his order to butchering by the bayonet; to save the labor of digging the vast grave needed to bury so many bodies, he had had the Mamelukes slaughtered in groups on the riverbank, so that they could simply be pushed into the river after the bayoneting.

This was the man who had devastated half the world in pursuit of his ambition to rule it, and the army now encamped across the valley had been shaped and organized to become the ideal instrument of his will. Toughened by a lifetime of warfare, and expert in the field, its soldiers were inspired by the presence of their Emperor, and were commanded by a set of officers who, to a man, had risen from their ranks. Low-born, often ill-educated, the French officers, from marshals down, were professional soldiers, pure and simple—brave, ambitious, and capable, at the tactical level at least. Many of them had risen from common private soldiers to become generals or marshals; some had even been made dukes, princes, or kings in the make-believe kingdoms and peerages created by Napoleon. Whatever their pretensions, they owed everything to the man who now led them, and they could be counted on to fight for him with their customary competence and courage.

The British soldiers now bivouacking all about De Lancey made up an entirely different sort of army, motivated by an entirely different set of values. While they agreed on what had to be done—Boney had to be defeated and the world rid of his menace—they were by no means crusaders. An unpretentious lot, they would have been embarrassed by the emotional posturings and protestations of the French, with their constant references to "glory" and their shouts of "*Vive l'Empereur!*" They were concerned only with getting the job done, and in spite of their great respect and regard for "Old Nosey," their commander, and their confidence that he would lead them in giving the French yet another good thrashing on the morrow, they would never dream of giving him the sort of worship the French accorded Napoleon. Recruited mostly from the shires of a still largely rural England and from the primitive villages of the Scottish Highlands, with a few "hard cases" from the cities and towns, they had been shaped into an efficient force by brutal army discipline and were led, not by professional officers like the French, but by amateurs drawn almost entirely from the country-gentleman class.

As an American, De Lancey enjoyed a peculiar status in British life, both military and civilian, since he could not be classified in the rigid English hierarchical system. He had thus been able to move freely through the British social structure, mingling with people at every level, from the highest to the lowest, and been accepted as an equal by all. This social mobility had given him a perspective and a rare perception of the nuances of British society. He was able to understand the peculiar English distrust of large standing armies led by professional officers, an aversion dating back to the days of Oliver Cromwell and the Protectorate, when the country had been taken over and run by a military clique. Wellington's army was rooted in the country, each regiment recruited in a single county or region and presided over by the same country squires to whom its men were accustomed in civil life to offer deference and from whom they received, in return, protection, advice, and assistance. It was, on the face of it, an infamous system whereby young men whose only qualification lay in their "gentle" birth purchased their commissions and exercised the responsibilities of command for which they had received little, if any, formal training, but, as De Lancey knew by experience, it worked surprisingly well. Trained from birth to ride, shoot, and have an eye for the lie of the land, and accustomed to assume responsibility for the welfare of those under them, these young country gentlemen quickly adapted to army life, and their strong behavioral code with its notions of personal honor gave them an integrity unlike anything to be found among their French counterparts. A British army, particularly when campaigning in neutral or friendly country, made a fetish of always paying its way, buying its supplies instead of simply seizing them, as the French did. Although as an American he sometimes found their pretensions amusing, De Lancey enjoyed these amateur officers and was proud to be of their company.

Satisfied that the regiments were where they should be and would be in their proper places for the confrontation tomorrow, De Lancey rode back through the gathering dusk to the village of Waterloo and to the spartan meal and truckle bed that awaited him there.

About midnight, as he slept the sleep of exhaustion in a crowded, dingy room, it began to rain. All that long night the rain poured down in a series of heavy showers that drenched the fields, flooded ditches, and turned the shallow valley into a muddy quagmire. For the thousands of men bivouacking in the open, the rain meant utter misery, quenching all but the biggest and best-tended fires, soaking through blankets and uniforms, reducing all but the best-chosen campsites to swamps. Yet, surprisingly, most of the soldiers in both armies slept on peacefully enough, their heads on their haversacks, a thin blanket or two above them keeping off some of the rain, and oblivious in their exhaustion to the wretchedness of their surroundings. They lay there still when a gray dawn brought the showers to an end and suffused the scene with a pink light and the promise of a better day. It was Sunday, June 18, 1815.

De Lancey was up and dressed by five o'clock, like the other staff officers billeted at the Waterloo inn and in the little chapel across the road, but, early as they were, their chief was up and about even earlier. Wellington had been writing orders and dispatches since three o'clock but seemed alert and rested when he joined his officers in the crowded breakfast room for a brisk and cheerful meal. Sharp on six o'clock he rode out on Copenhagen and clattered down the cobblestones in the midst of his staff to tour his hilltop battle line.

His appearance and his cheerful and confident manner acted like a tonic on all who saw him, officers and men alike. There were cheers from groups of men gathered about their smoky fires, cooking breakfast or drying clothing, and even the wettest recruit, dismally cleaning his weapons and equipment in a muddy bivouac, looked up with a grin or a cheery wave as the Duke rode by. The "long-nosed bugger who always beat the French" could be counted on to do so again today. Every man, all the thousands who would stand in the Allied line, had the opportunity of seeing at close hand the leader who would direct their destiny this day. Riding beside Wellington as he made his way slowly through the awakening regiments, De Lancey was impressed yet again by the close affinity between leader and led, by the curious mutual sympathy that seemed to link this abrupt, undemonstrative man with this rough, workmanlike army.

As they made their way along the ridge, stopping at each

regimental encampment for a word with its officers, the Duke and his staff were joined by senior officers from the Allied nations: Alava from Spain, Muffling from Prussia, Baron Vincent of Austria, and Pozzo di Borgo, a Corsican who represented, of all people, the Tsar of Russia. The party was now some forty strong, larger than Wellington would have liked. When the Duke of Richmond, a civilian, and his fifteen-year-old son attempted to join it, the Duke called out: "William, you ought to be in bed. Duke, you have no business here!" But he could do nothing about the others, which included, besides his own staff, a swarm of aides attached to the other general officers. They rode on, a jingling cavalcade, bright and cheerful as if going to a fashionable hunt, and, despite his own preoccupations, De Lancey found himself enjoying their chatter.

When he had finished his tour of the Allied line, Wellington took up a position beneath a large elm tree in the southwest corner of the Mont St. Jean crossroads which, with this prominent landmark and central location, made an ideal forward command post with good views over the whole battlefront. He was content with what he saw and confident that his mixed bag of men was disposed to best advantage.

His purpose was clear. The nature of his army, with much of its manpower quite inexperienced and some of it of dubious quality and staying power, meant that he could not play the part of the attacker in the coming battle; his army, or most of it, was no match for the French veterans in maneuvering ability. He must fight a defensive battle and make the most of a strong defensive position. His object was to hold this position until the Prussians arrived; Blücher had sent him a message during the night promising to march at first light so as to arrive early in the afternoon. Accordingly, he had few worries about his left flank, the direction from which the Prussians would come, and was content to base it on the farmhouse of

Papelotte. He had packed this strongpoint with his young Nassau soldiers, hoping that the thick walls of the farm would give them the confidence needed to stand up to the French attack. Certainly, being out on the flank, behind cover, and with Prussian help on its way, it was the safest place for them. The other two walled farms in front of the ridge were likely to come under the heaviest attack and, accordingly, the Duke garrisoned them with his best and steadiest troops, sending the British Foot Guards into Hougoumont and the King's German Legion, an élite unit, into La Haye Sainte. To guard his right flank, which Wellington regarded as his most vulnerable point, and the key to his communications with Brussels, he stationed a strong force of 17,000 men behind his line at the hamlet of Hal, to act as a reserve. The rest of his army he strung out along the top of the ridge, the infantry and artillery just behind the crest, the cavalry in the rear, where it could be brought up to support as required.

The Duke had discussed these allocations previously with De Lancey, and the two now talked over improvements and amendments as they made their final adjustments to the battle line.

By nine o'clock the Allied army was in position and ready for action; its men had cleaned their weapons, clearing their muskets first by firing them off into the air in a sustained popping and a cloud of powder smoke. They were now drying their uniforms in the strong morning sunshine, with its promise of a warm day to come.

But across the valley Napoleon, who had built his reputation on quick, decisive action, was again procrastinating, as he had tended to do in his recent battles. He seemed lethargic, unable to make up his mind; he was also suffering from piles, which made it painful for him to ride his horse. In any event, he failed to take advantage of the early-morning hours. He refused to believe his brother Jérôme's information about Blücher intending to meet

Wellington here, and insisted instead that the Prussians were in full retreat for home. Despite the strength of Wellington's position, he planned a straightforward frontal attack, and when some of his commanders, notably Soult and Reille (who had fought the Duke in Spain and knew the quality of British infantry), advised flank attacks instead, he poured scorn on their caution.

"Just because you have been beaten by Wellington, you think he's a good general. I tell you, Wellington is a bad general, the English are bad troops, and this affair is nothing more than eating breakfast."

The precious minutes ticked away—minutes in which Napoleon could have confronted Wellington's army, still unsupported by the Prussians—and with them passed this opportunity of defeating the Allies separately. Napoleon decided to delay still further, "to give the ground time to dry out," as he explained to his staff. He would hold a review of his army, both to exhilarate his own troops and to intimidate those of the Allies across the valley.

Standing on a low knoll in front of the inn, La Belle Alliance, that marked the center of the French hilltop line, one hand thrust inside his greatcoat in a familiar posture, the Emperor reviewed his troops in full view of the Allied army lounging at ease across the way. In consternation and disbelief at first, then with growing admiration, Wellington's infantry watched the spectacle unfold, as the most gorgeously uniformed army the world had ever seen paraded its splendors before its leader.

It was a stunning sight, overwhelming both by numbers—some 70,000 men marched past to the music of their bands—and by the magnificence and color of the various regimental uniforms. The grenadiers of the Old Guard marched steadily in their somber campaign blues, reserving the dress uniforms in their blanket rolls for a triumphal entry into Brussels, but in their tall bearskins and bristling mustaches they were a formidable sight, and their thunderous "*Vive l'Empereur!*" could be heard above the music of their band by their British counterparts, the Foot Guards, waiting in Hougoumont.

But it was the French cavalry who made the most splendid show: dragoons with brass helmets over tigerskin turbans; hussars with gold-frogged dolmans, tight pantaloons in every color of the rainbow, plumed shakos, and fur-trimmed pelisses gay in the bright morning sunshine; lancers in scarlet, with pennons fluttering at their lance points, and sabretaches and plastrons gleaming with gold-laced embroidery; cuirassiers in glittering breastplates, their steel helmets crested with copper and topped by horsehair manes; chasseurs in crimson and green; carabiniers in dazzling white and gold. Everywhere the sun twinkled from gold and silver crests, badges and accoutrements, or from spurs and sabers set off by rich saddlecloths of leopardskin, embroidered broadcloth, or fleece.

The spectacle filled the Allies with awed admiration. British infantrymen nudged one another as the brilliant procession crossed the slopes of the hill opposite, and felt proud to be taking on such magnificent adversaries. But if the review failed to daunt the enemy, it at least achieved Napoleon's other purpose—it bound his army to him with renewed enthusiasm, and infused it with an exhilarating eagerness to attack. Two very different leaders had exerted their personal charisma to inspire two very different armies: the British, dour and determined to defend, the French, uplifted and thirsting to attack.

To De Lancey, it seemed most appropriate that two such contrasting armies should contest the future of Europe; the one representing kings and parliaments, the other an imperial tyranny. But he had enough sense not to raise the point with his brother officers, who were looking forward to the battle as a sort of sporting contest where one matched strength and skill with a respected opponent, with life itself put at hazard.

In any event, he was still the busiest man on Wellington's staff, as he undertook to clear the battlefield of any unnecessary clutter. Commissary carts, which had brought supplies to the troops the previous day, were packed off to Brussels, and with them he had sent off all the camp followers of one kind and another, and the inevitable collection of curious civilians who had ventured out from the city and suburbs. He hoped that the last of the supply wagons would depart the encampment in time to leave the vital Brussels road clear for military use, but the wagons were slow and there were constant delays; his own staff officers were kept busy sorting out the endless tangles.

It was just after ten o'clock when De Lancey noticed some untoward movement among troops stationed near the farm of Hougoumont on the Allied right, and drew it to the attention of Wellington as they rode along the crest of the ridge. A Belgian battalion, stationed in the orchard in support of the farmhouse strongpoint, had become restless as the French forces gathered on the opposite hillside. Young and inexperienced and more familiar with the French Emperor than with the English Duke who now led them, they had become panicky as the seemingly endless parade of French military might had unfolded across the valley, and some of them were now beginning to desert their posts and make for the rear. It was obvious that if something was not done quickly the entire battalion would dissolve before a shot was even fired, and the panic might soon spread to other units in the Allied line.

Instantly the Duke put spurs to his horse and, with De Lancey at his side, galloped down the slope, drawing rein in the midst of the frightened young conscripts. With a few well-chosen words in his execrable French, and much waving of his hat, he managed to rally them and, after addressing himself to their commander, a fresh-faced, excitable youngster, he was able to get them returned to their position. But not all of the disgruntled unit were persuaded by the Duke's exhortations. A few of the angrier, or more frightened, soldiers began waving their muskets in threatening gestures as their comrades bore them back to their lines. Convinced that their officer now had them in charge, Wellington chose to ignore these dissidents, but as the Duke turned his horse about to ride away, De Lancey saw, out of the corner of his eye, several muskets suddenly leveled, aimed right at Wellington's back. He gave a sudden shout: "Look out!"

As the startled Copenhagen shied, the muskets went off. One of the balls narrowly missed Wellington's shoulder and the others whistled harmlessly overhead. The Duke made no response of any kind but rode on, his face impassive as ever, and the angry De Lancey had no choice but to follow him. As they rode back to the crossroads, Wellington made his only comment.

"Well, De Lancey, it is with these, and such as these, that we must win the battle."

8
A Sea of Horsemen

JUST AFTER TEN O'CLOCK, as his staff sat their horses all about him, Wellington's keen eye detected movement far on the eastern horizon, beyond his left flank. With his glass he could make out a dark line just below the smudge of woodland known as Paris Wood, and, as he watched, he saw that the line was moving. Far away, a column of men was marching out of the trees, a column that could only be the Prussian advance guard, but it was still many miles distant. Snapping his telescope shut, the Duke turned to his staff and, in a satisfied manner, said: "Here comes old Blücher. He'll be with us in no time."

His confident manner and cheerful bearing reassured any faint hearts among his distinguished foreign guests, but, as attention turned elsewhere, De Lancey caught the eye of the Earl of Uxbridge and they exchanged a thoughtful glance. Both of them had also seen that dark, distant column and both had realized, as Wellington must have done, that it could not possibly reach the field of battle for many hours. It would be dusk at least, and the battle lost or won, before it could intervene. Whatever Wellington might say for the benefit of the Allied leaders, he knew, as De Lancey and Uxbridge now knew, that the issue must be decided by the forces now on the field.

What they did not know was that a French force of

33,000 men under Marshal Grouchy had been detached from the main French army specifically to prevent any Prussian intervention; nor did they know that Napoleon's indecision and Soult's poor staff work would keep Grouchy marching and countermarching far from the battlefield on which he might have played a decisive role.

Now that he had seen his troops properly in position and ready for the coming battle, Wellington swung down from his horse and accepted a cup of tea, offered to him by an infantry private from an enormous fire-blackened pot sitting in the embers of a bivouac fire. In spite of his narrow escape from the mutinous Belgians, and the unsettling indications it offered about the state of some of his forces, the Duke seemed poised and confident. His cheerful banter with the infantryman about the quality of his tea brought laughter from his staff and relaxed any tensions that might have been felt on the morning of this momentous day.

Young De Lancey himself, for all that he had no illusions about the availability of the Prussians or the quality of some of the Allied regiments, felt a quiet confidence in the outcome of the day. They were established in a strong position, one he had chosen himself, and no one knew better how to make the most of it than his commander-in-chief. Wellington was the ablest commander Britain had produced since Marlborough, a proven leader who could be depended upon to get the most from his men, and a tactical genius who had beaten every French general he had faced. He was at the height of his powers, a commander one could be prepared to die for—an eventuality that might be all too imminent, De Lancey reflected wryly, with a glance at the magnificent parade just ending across the valley.

Napoleon was something of an enigma. De Lancey did not share the prevailing view of his brother officers, who regarded Bonaparte as a bumptious little upstart with a flair for warfare, and he recognized the undoubted organizing genius and dynamism of a man who could bleed a nation dry and still hold its adoration. But ever since Borodino three years before, when the Russians had fought him to a standstill in a bloody stand-up battle, there had been doubts about the Emperor's military talents. The appalling catastrophe of the Russian campaign, when his misjudgements and indecision had thrown away almost a million men, had been followed by a series of battles seemingly fought by rote, with Napoleon content to allow his subordinates to run the battlefield according to an inflexible formula. The Emperor had grown fat and flabby, his manner increasingly dilatory and indecisive, yet he still commanded the loyalty of his army. Would that loyalty be enough to help him win?

Looking about him, at the British regiments lounging comfortably in their positions, dry and rested, who a few hours before had been soaked and uncertain and vulnerable, De Lancey rather thought not. Time was Napoleon's enemy, and he was still frittering precious hours away in parades and posturing when he should have been making the most of them to achieve a victory he could not afford to lose. Surely he could not procrastinate much longer; the last of the resplendent regiments across the way had passed in review, and a warm sun had dried the ground; the two armies now faced each other in growing impatience.

Never before in the history of Europe had there been such a concentration of force. Wellington, with just over 67,000 men and 156 guns, faced Napoleon's 72,000 men and 246 guns; a total of almost 140,000 men and more than 400 guns, together with some 30,000 horses, were jammed into a battle area of less than three square miles. Such dense masses of men, such concentrated firepower, made one thing at least certain: the coming battle would be a bloody one.

At exactly 11:25 a.m. the traditional nine cannon shots, in three groups of three, sounded the beginning of the French attack, and it began with a tremendous cannonade, another hallmark of a Napoleonic battle. Within minutes much of the French hillside was obscured by clouds of powder smoke. Soon the Allied positions, too, were wreathed in black smoke, pierced by stabbing jets of flame as the Allied artillery replied. Wellington had positioned his artillery in batteries between the regiments spread along his hillside, and the guns were strongly entrenched behind embrasures cut into thick hedgemounds.

Much of the French fire was concentrated on Hougoumont, and it was to that strongpoint that Wellington, with De Lancey at his side, galloped first. As cannonballs bounced through the fields in front of them, the Guards in the orchard lay down on the ground in response to a bugle call, and, as the shot flew ever faster and closer, De Lancey found himself wishing he could do the same.

But the Duke, impassive as ever, paid little heed to the hail of metal all about him, and Copenhagen showed equal composure. Aware that the French planned something for Hougoumont, Wellington positioned himself on the slope immediately to the rear of the fortified farmhouse, so that he could personally direct its defense. Swarms of skirmishers could be seen through the clouds of gunsmoke, making their way down the hillside and up the Allied slopes, taking advantage of every bit of available cover. They flitted through the scattered woodland at the valley bottom and up across a patch of open country into the orchard itself, where a bloody battle soon developed with outlying sections of the Guards. But as De Lancey watched, he became aware of the main thrust of the French attack. A column of blue-coated infantry, four regiments strong and all veterans, loomed through the smoke, marching steadily on the farmhouse. On they came, through the orchard, driving the Guards before them, and on to the walls of the farmhouse itself.

The rearguard had entered the north gate, closing the tall wooden doors behind them. A gigantic French subaltern, armed with an axe, stove in a panel of the heavy gate, lifted the bar that held it shut, and led a wave of wildly cheering attackers into the paved courtyard in the very center of the position. For a heart-stopping moment it seemed that Hougoumont, a strong position garrisoned by the steadiest Allied troops, might fall in the very first attack upon it. But the Guards within fought back with no loss of composure, and five burly Coldstreamers—four officers and a sergeant, De Lancey could see—cut their way to the gateway through which the French were streaming and, hurling themselves against the huge door, forced it closed again, inch by inch, despite the pressure from the Frenchmen outside striving to get in. The gate was shut, then barred into position. Now the garrison turned its attention to the attackers in the courtyard. Assailed now from all sides, the French fought valiantly but, one by one, were cut down until only a drummer boy remained standing. Left all alone, the boy hurled his drum, his only weapon, at the circle of guardsmen all about him. De Lancey watched while a British corporal led the sobbing boy to a seat beside an outbuilding, where he was soon joined by the wounded men of both sides, laid out in an orderly row. The Duke, on his hillside vantage point, turned a somber face toward his aide.

"By God, De Lancey," he exclaimed, "if those brave fellows hadn't managed to close those gates, we could all have been dished!"

But the attackers, though rebuffed, were not defeated; from the cover of the orchard they poured a withering fire on the farmhouse walls, and as fresh troops arrived they redoubled their efforts to get inside. Sizing up the situation, Wellington resolved upon a risky solution. He sent word to a battery of British howitzers, which he had previously sited nearby in support of the farm, to lob shrapnel shell over the heads of the Hougoumont defenders, to fall upon the French in the orchard beyond. The battery opened fire, a hail of exploding steel fell upon the French, and in a matter of minutes the attack was brought to a standstill. A surge of British defenders, pouring out from their walled enclosure, soon swept the orchard and adjoining fields clear, and once again the entire position was restored to Allied control.

But the French were not done with Hougoumont. Their general, Jérôme Bonaparte, had been ordered by his brother, the Emperor, to feint at the farmhouse in order to mask a concerted attack upon the Allied center, but the rebuff of his veterans had fired his spirt: what had been intended as a gesture now became a full-blooded assault. A mass of fresh troops, more veteran infantrymen from Foy's division, were sent forward to the attack. Thousands of blue-coated grenadiers poured down the slope and across the valley towards the embattled farmhouse. Wellington's response was typical. Not wishing to use any more men than were absolutely necessary, he sent down only four extra companies of his Guards, urging them on their way with the instructions: "There, my lads, in with you; let me see no more of you!"

The French attack swept up to the farmhouse woods, and lapped about the walls, but could go no further. A furious fire poured from every embrasure and from the upper windows of the farmhouse itself, while the howitzers on the hillside behind lobbed a steady stream of shrapnel into the massed attackers. The French faltered, and hung back, but still Jérôme would not let go. More and more men were poured into the attack, until the best part of two French divisions were heavily engaged with one British brigade. For an hour and a half the battle raged, the French infantry ranging all around, in firm control of fields and orchards but unable to take the farm itself. Hougoumont, it was now clear, was impregnable so long as its garrison's ammunition held out. It was time for the Duke to turn his attention elsewhere, and he and De Lancey rode back to the crossroads and his elm-tree command post.

At about the same time, on the slope opposite, Napoleon first caught sight of the distant dark line emerging from the Paris Wood far to his right, and recognized it at once for what it was: the advance guard of Blücher's Prussians. Immediately he dispatched the whole of Lobau's Corps and two divisions of cavalry to reinforce Grouchy, with instructions to keep the Prussians from intervening, but his orders were couched in such vague and misleading language that Grouchy was left in an agony of baffled frustration.

What with the forces now sent from the field and the thousands of prime infantrymen committed to the increasingly pointless assaults upon Hougoumont, Napoleon had now tied up more than two-thirds of his entire force and wasted eight hours of precious daylight, yet at the end of an hour and a half of furious fighting he had nothing at all to show for it. In a fit of pique he turned the direction of the battle over to Marshal Ney, and moved forward from his quarters at Rossomme to the inn at La Belle Alliance, where he established himself in a comfortable armchair and moodily sat back to watch Ney's work unfold.

It began with a tremendous cannonade by a battery of no fewer than eighty-four guns, twenty-four of them the terrible twelve-pounders referred to by Napoleon as his "beautiful, wicked daughters." The guns concentrated exclusively on the left wing of the Allied line. Yet although the shot flew like hail over the hillside, leaving balls stuck everywhere in the soft ground like so many hailstones, it did little damage to troops lying down on the reverse slope, out of harm's way, although a force of Dutch and Belgians commanded by General Bylandt were caught on the exposed hillside and suffered heavily.

After a half-hour of furious cannonading, a dark mass of French infantry moved down the slopes, 16,000 of them from D'Erlon's corps. All veteran soldiers, they marched with steady precision across the valley, out of the smoke of the French batteries, which suddenly fell silent, and up the hillside toward the orchards and buildings of La Haye Sainte and the left of the Allied position. One division advanced in line, the other three were in dense phalanxes, packed shoulder to shoulder in formations two hundred files wide and twenty-four to twenty-seven deep. They moved inexorably up the slope, through the orchards, lapping around the farm buildings like a dark sea engulfing rocks, driving the German defenders from the woods and cutting off La Haye Sainte from the rest of the Allied position. As the Duke and his staff watched anxiously, it seemed that the farm itself, the key to their left flank, must be overrun, but its German Legion garrison fought with valor and maintained their hold on their isolated stronghold as the French tide flowed on past. As the dark wave crested the hill, it crashed into Bylandt's light division of French and Belgian conscripts, already badly shaken by the cannonade they had experienced in their exposed position, which had killed or wounded all their senior officers. Lacking firm direction, the youngsters simply loosed off a scattered volley and took to their heels before the advancing French, making for the nearby woods and being roundly booed by the Cameron Highlanders behind them as they ran past.

But the British were old hands at coping with the French columns they had encountered so often before. The long red lines poured a devastating fire into the dense masses before them, volley after precise volley at close range. Only the front two ranks of the French formations could reply and, as they topped the ridge and were exposed to the full impact of the waiting British lines, the packed masses of men came to an abrupt halt, while musketry and cannon fire from a hilltop battery tore great rents and gaps in them. And at this critical moment Picton's Highlanders decided the issue. Waved on by their indomitable commander, the Scots, all 1,400 of them, flung themselves on the mass before them in a furious counterattack. Through his telescope De Lancey watched Sir Thomas Picton himself, waving his sword, cheering his men forward, but at that very moment he saw the general's celebrated top hat, worn to protect his defective eyes, knocked from his head, and the gallant general toppled to the ground, a bullet through his brow.

Howling for revenge, his Highlanders flung themselves again at the yielding ranks before them, their long bayonets glittering in the sun as their line surged forward. A devastating volley, poured in at close range by Halkett's brigade, brought another French phalanx to a stop as it crested the hill beyond the savage Scots, yet the solid mass of Frenchmen behind pushed the dark mass slowly forward again. The sheer numbers of French soldiers threatened to overwhelm the attenuated British line, and, lowering his glass, De Lancey looked towards the Duke.

"The heavies?" he asked, and Wellington replied with a brief nod. A galloper was sent instantly with an order to the British cavalry waiting impatiently behind the Allied left wing, and the Duke, with only De Lancey and Somerset in attendance, rode out in his wake. They arrived as the regiments—the Life Guards, the Blues, and the Royal Scots Greys—were already trotting forward. Standing up in his stirrups and waving his hat, Wellington called out to them in his clear, resonant voice: "Now, gentlemen, for the honor of the household troops!"

It was all that was needed to add impetus to the charge. With a great shout of "Scotland Forever!" the leading regiment, the Scots Greys, put spurs to their horses and swept down upon the struggling mass of infantry before them.

Their cheer was answered by wild yells of encouragement from the Camerons and Gordons as the great gray horses thundered through them, knocking aside foot soldiers, friend and enemy alike, as they cleaved their way through. Some of the Gordons caught at the reins as the horses shouldered through them, and were borne with them into the swirling fray in front. Like a thunderbolt the torrent of men and horses crashed into the French phalanxes, the troopers rising in their stirrups to gain greater force for their whirling saber strokes.

To De Lancey, the charge of the Household Brigade seemed like some elemental force of nature; the very ground shook beneath him and the wind of their passing brushed his cheek as the torrent of magnificent horses and glittering riders surged past. Nothing could resist that tremendous weight of horses and men. With a shattering crash the heavy cavalry met the head of the French column, overbore it, and cut its way through the thick files behind, to the cry of "On to Paris!"

A company of Life Guards fell upon a troop of French cuirassiers operating on the flanks of their infantry column; De Lancey could hear the clash of their sabers upon the French breastplates and helmets and watched, appalled, as a big trooper cut through a French helmet with such violence that the face fell from the head like a bit of sliced apple.

Under this furious assault the French columns shivered to a halt, then simply dissolved, as individual soldiers, then groups of two or three, sought to escape the terrible horsemen. In seconds, the solid formations had become an amorphous mass of struggling individuals, pouring back down the slopes toward the safety of their own lines across the valley, pursued by a yelling wall of vengeful cavalrymen.

At the bottom of the slope the British buglers sounded

the Rally; De Lancey could hear the staccato notes high above the tumult of battle, but the wave of men and horses surged on, caught up in the mad exhilaration of the charge as they swept all before them. It was like Spain all over again, thought De Lancey, as he felt a sickening wrench of apprehension in his stomach—the same old story of dash and élan, coupled with lack of discipline, which always bedeviled British cavalry.

With mingled admiration and despair he watched as the scarlet squadrons spurred, unchecked, up the slopes opposite, cutting their way through all who opposed them. He saw one eagle standard, then another, snatched by troopers from swirling masses of infantrymen, and then the tide of red coats and shining steel swept into the great battery in the center of the French position. The hatred and frustration felt by men who had had to endure the frightful cannonade from these guns could be seen in the fury of the British assault. Again and again the sabers rose and fell as the gunners were cut to pieces; through his glass De Lancey could see horsemen even slashing at the very guns and limbers with their swords. But he could see, too, the masses of French infantry and cavalry moving down into the valley on either side of the Household Brigade. In a matter of moments it was cut off, with a wall of Frenchmen between it and the British lines. Their fury spent, the troopers rallied now in response to their buglers and furious commanders. The regiments reformed and faced about to confront their new enemy. Again the bugles sounded the charge, and they fell on the mass of blue uniforms below them.

But it was too much; the horses were blown, many of their riders wounded and arm-weary and the charge lacked the impetus of the initial assault. De Lancey watched sadly as they were cut down and swallowed up by the swarming Frenchmen all about them. Colonel

Ponsonby of the Scots Greys was last seen leading his men, with both arms shot through, holding his reins clenched in his teeth. A few score troopers, battered and bleeding, regained the safety of their lines, but most of them were killed or captured. The heavy brigade, the pride of the Allied cavalry, had almost ceased to exist. On the other hand, it had taken with it an entire infantry division and eliminated the threat to the vulnerable left flank. Wellington snapped shut his telescope and turned his attention elsewhere with his customary composure, as he rode back to his crossroads position. As he passed the remnants of the Life Guards, walking their blown horses toward the rear, he raised his hat in salute and called out, "Guards! I thank you!" without a word of reproach.

With De Lancey at his side, he returned just in time to witness an alarming sight. It was sharp on three o'clock, De Lancey noted with a glance at his watch, when they reached the elm-tree post and looked out to see Hougoumont a mass of flames. In silence they watched as barns, outbuildings, and the great house itself were wreathed in flame. A concentrated torrent of howitzer shells had poured into it from the French batteries, and had set first a haystack, and then the thatched roofs of some outbuildings, on fire. The blaze swept through building after building, burning to death all the wounded of both sides laid out helpless on their floors. The beleaguered garrison was forced out of doors by the fire, but concentrated its efforts in attempts to save the main house. De Lancey could see the bucket line passing water from the farmyard well into the house, but the efforts seemed puny in the face of the towering flames. And yet, by a kind of miracle the fire, after making a clean sweep of the surrounding buildings, was brought to a halt, appropriately enough in front of the chapel. It might have been a change of wind as much as the efforts of the garrison that finally halted it, but whatever the cause, it gave the Duke, on his vantage point overlooking the site, hope that the position, the key to his center, might still be held. He sent a message of encouragement to the smoke-blackened soldiers who were now taking up positions in the chapel and any other places within the walls that were still tenable.

Grueling though the ordeal at Hougoumont had been, it was as nothing compared with the storm that now engulfed the Allied left and center. The whole of the French artillery, save for a battery or two beyond reasonable range, now concentrated their fire on Wellington's left flank. Napoleon was determined to crush the Allied left before Blücher's Prussians could intervene. The roar of the guns was incessant, and the rain of shot and shrapnel was devastating; the British infantry, although screened behind the crest of the hill, was decimated. They lay on the ground, but there was no escaping that remorseless fire. Wellington was forced to order a withdrawal of a hundred yards to the rear, where a scattered wood gave some protection, but his troops were suffering terribly.

A steady stream of wounded found its way to the rear, mixed with an occasional deserter shamming an injury. A whole regiment of Hanoverian horse, a "social" regiment recruited from young gentlemen of family, now took to its heels and bolted from the field, spreading alarm and bogus news of a French victory all the way to Brussels. Still the cannonade continued. Seeking what meager shelter they could find, the Allied infantry clung to their hilltop position, while all about them the world went mad. An Allied ammunition dump in the rear blew up, the detonation scarce heard amid the constant roar of the French guns, and sent a towering column of smoke high above the hillside. For nearly half an hour the ordeal went on, the mightiest sustained cannonade the world had ever known. Yet, at the end, Wellington's line, though thinned and shaken, retained its dominating position, and the Prussian columns had moved closer.

The time had now come for the French to make their all-out bid for victory, and, encouraged by a glimpse of

Wellington's withdrawal on his left flank, Napoleon ordered Ney to concentrate his attack on the Allied left and center.

Just before four o'clock De Lancey, who, with Somerset and Colonel James Stanhope, was alone in attendance on the Duke (the remainder of the staff having dispersed into smaller groups as Wellington considered they offered too large and tempting a target for the French gunners), caught sight of a shimmer amid the dense clouds of smoke that masked the French position, and a moment later drew in his breath at the sight that now emerged. A great glittering line of men and horses, stretching in an unbroken rank from Hougoumont all the way to La Haye Sainte, rode slowly out of the swirling gunsmoke, moving steadily across the valley and up the Allied hillside. The sun glinted from helmets, cuirasses, sabers, and accoutrements as the cavalry emerged from the mists and fog of war, a thing of terrible beauty. More than 4,000 horsemen, led by Marshal Ney himself, rode stirrup to stirrup across the valley, increasing their pace to a trot as they approached the Allied hillside. Up, up they came, and on the hilltop the infantry regiments made ready for them.

"Prepare to receive cavalry!"

At the order, each regiment formed itself into a hollow square, three ranks deep, the outer rank kneeling with the butts of their muskets placed firmly on the ground and their long bayonets presenting a fence of long, sharp points to keep horsemen at bay, while the inner two ranks stood with leveled muskets, awaiting the word of command to fire into their close-packed assailants. The gunners in front had abandoned their guns as the enemy drew nearer, removing a wheel from each piece so that the French could not take it away, and bowling it before them as they sought shelter in the center of the squares.

In a great dark wave crested with gleaming steel, the

sea of French cavalry broke in fury upon the Allied squares. Screaming horses reared and shied as they confronted the serried bayonets. Their shouting, cursing riders swung their sabers as they strove to come to closer quarters, and then the terrible volleys crashed out, again and again and again. The surging masses of horses and men about each square were shredded by the withering fire poured into them. De Lancey could actually hear the impact as a thousand heavy musketballs crashed through armor or thudded into flesh. Nothing could withstand that inexorable British musketry. Ney's cavalry just melted away, leaving behind a mound of dead and wounded, horses and men, all about each square.

But this had been simply the first assault; already across the valley a new wave, twice as strong, was trotting to the attack. Ney had poured 8,000 men, in two solid columns, into this second onslaught; more than 5,000 of them were fresh men on unblown horses. On they came, up the slopes, as the Allied infantry watched with a jaundiced eye.

"Here come those bloody fools again!" muttered one grizzled veteran to his mate at De Lancey's elbow, as the splendid phalanxes rode toward them. The attack was delivered with even greater force, the troopers riding their mounts fearlessly right up to the bayonet fence and cutting at anything they could reach. De Lancey watched one mustachioed cuirassier, unable to penetrate beyond the hedge of bayonets, sheathe his saber and draw his pistol, discharging it at point-blank range at a sergeant in the second rank. The man fell dead, whereupon the Frenchman flung the empty weapon with all his force at the nearest British soldier before turning and riding disdainfully away. Yet for all the bravery of individual horsemen, all the élan and dash of squadron and regiment and the mounting piles of dead and wounded around each square, the surging assaults of this magnificent cavalry broke upon the solid British squares with as little effect as waves crashing on a rockbound shore. The French won a momentary success on the left flank, where a Dutch-Belgian unit received a charge while in open order because of a mistaken command and were cut to pieces, but the gap was quickly filled, and, at the end of a dozen furious charges, the greatest sustained cavalry assault in European history, Wellington's indomitable infantry still clung to its ridge-top position, an unbroken wall between Napoleon and Brussels.

But at what a terrible cost, De Lancey thought, looking around at the carnage within the square where he stood beside the Duke. All about him were piled the dead and dying, pulled from the ranks by their comrades as they fell, along with the ghastly long rows of wounded lying untended. Everywhere was the smoke and din of battle, the reek of burnt gunpowder, the crash of musketry, the yells and oaths and moans of men at the very limits of endurance. The squares were smaller now, and their ranks thinner. The men who knelt or stood in them were desperate with the stress and fatigue of incessant fighting. It was nearly half past four, De Lancey saw, drawing out his watch. Most of these men had been in action for hours, fighting for their very lives under a hot sun; thirst was now a factor, as well as weariness, as the last precious drops from upturned canteens were emptied. This was an army, De Lancey sensed, that had been pushed as far as it could go.

But no one knew this better than the Duke. Seeing De Lancey pull out his watch, he inquired the time and, on being told, declared: "The battle is mine, and if the Prussians arrive soon, there will be an end of the war!"

He now set about to transmit this confidence to his men. With his little knot of staff officers at his side, he trotted again along the ridgetop, visiting each battered square and chatting with its weary officers and men as they rested before the next assault. There was horror aplenty here: men with limbs half severed by cavalry sabers, or dreadfully mangled by shrapnel, piles of corpses, wounded horses screaming in agony. Yet the spirit of the men was surprisingly good, and, after a word or two with the Duke, they took on a new animation and were soon talking, and even grimly joking, about their own exploits.

At the end of his line Wellington turned Copenhagen about, but before they could return to the crossroads a new sound brought him and his officers to an abrupt halt. There it was again. Far away still, out there near the Paris Wood, the sound of distant gunfire. No mere musketry this, but the deep, full-throated rumble of artillery. It could only be Blücher's guns. Somewhere out there the Prussians were in action against Napoleon's flank, and the Duke and his staff looked at one another with silent surmise.

9
Victory

AT HIS POST IN FRONT of La Belle Alliance, Napoleon, too, had heard the Prussian guns and knew what they portended. Unless the British were crushed quickly, he would soon be facing two undefeated armies, one in front and one on his flank. In agitation he got up from his chair and paced back and forth, head sunk forward in thought, while across the valley Ney resumed his assault, this time with a mixed force of infantry and horse artillery in addition to yet more cavalry. As they had all afternoon, the French columns reached the top of the ridge and galloped about the embattled Allied squares, but, after long minutes of furious fighting, they recoiled and came streaming back down to the valley floor, followed by a nearly demented Ney. The marshal was out of his mind with frustration and fighting frenzy. Clearly it was time for the Emperor to intervene.

A glance at his watch showed how time had been wasted; it was now going on for six o'clock, and darkness—and the Prussians—would soon be here. When Ney himself finally appeared before him, the Emperor was ready with clear-cut orders for him. Capture La Haye Sainte at all costs, and do it with everything that could be spared: horse, foot, guns. Ney, hatless and streaming with sweat, having had half a dozen horses shot out from under him, looked across the valley at the battered farmhouse and nodded in understanding. Minutes later, his jaw set in determination, he led out yet another huge force, formed as before in two massive columns. It was six o'clock, and on both sides of the valley men knew that it was the moment of decision.

As the dark masses of the French surged across yet again, Wellington and his staff worked feverishly to strengthen the point of impact. De Lancey brought up the last of the reserve cavalry, and a force of mixed Brunswick and Hanoverian infantry was sent up to support the British squares on the left and center, now worn down to a fraction of their strength by a long afternoon of slaughter. Allied artillery pounded the oncoming columns, but the French mobile batteries opened fire in return, and soon La Haye Sainte was engulfed by an enormous mass of blue-coated infantrymen, swarming up the walls, pounding on the gates, while a cloud of horsemen drew the fire of the nearest British supporting squares.

The Allied line wavered, and the Duke himself had to rally a Brunswick regiment when it began to give ground. The frightened faces of the young conscripts, hardly more than boys, took confidence from their commander-in-chief's assured, brisk manner and turned back to face their enemy with something like composure. But as the defenders of La Haye Sainte poured a crippling fire from every loophole and embrasure, the hilltop squares kept up their steady volleys, and the British artillerymen served their guns with devastating effect, it seemed that the French attack was beginning to lose its momentum. And then, within a matter of seconds, everything seemed to fall apart.

As De Lancey and Somerset, awaiting the Duke's return to the crossroads, looked on, the fire from La Haye Sainte suddenly fell silent: the garrison had run out of ammunition! De Lancey realized what had happened. The King's German Legion needed special cartridges for their Baker rifles, and it must have been this ammunition that had gone up in smoke earlier in the battle. In the twinkling of an eye the French poured into the farmhouse, over the walls and through the riven gate. After a desperate hand-to-hand struggle in which almost the entire garrison was bayoneted, the vital outpost was theirs. At the same moment, the nearest hilltop square was overrun and the supporting Brunswick regiments were swept away by the fire of a French horse battery and a swarm of cuirassiers. After hours of fruitless pounding, a few dramatic moments had put the French in command of the vital Allied center and in a position to roll up Wellington's line in either direction and claim victory. French infantry poured in to garrison La Haye Sainte and a swarm of sharpshooters spread out along the slopes to shield them as they took up their position.

Suddenly the crossroads command post became the target of French fire. Uxbridge, anxiously conferring with Wellington, had his knee smashed by a ball, and called out: "By God, I've lost my leg!" The Duke, with a quick glance, responded: "By God, so you have!" Uxbridge had no sooner been led away to have the leg amputated than Fitzroy Somerset, riding close behind the Duke, lost his right arm to another musket ball. Wellington, who, as in all his battles, seemed to bear a charmed life, was left with only De Lancey in attendance from what had once seemed an over-large staff.

It was half past six, the French had established a foothold in the vital Allied center, and there was still no sign of the Prussians. The battle hung in the balance, and it was time for the Duke to show his greatness. After a hurried conference with De Lancey, the two rode off in opposite directions: De Lancey to round up a reserve division of Dutch-Belgian troops from Merbraine on the extreme right, together with every uncommitted soldier he could find from flank and rear, and Wellington to pour in everything that could be spared to support his threatened center and to rally and reorganize his bruised and battered squares. His very appearance was a tonic to his hard-pressed infantrymen, as were his few words, called out as he drew rein in their midst: "Wait a little longer, my lads, you shall have at them presently." To their officers he called: "Hard pounding, this, gentlemen; let us try who can pound the hardest." And to an old British county regiment: "Stand fast, we must not be beat. What will they say in England?"

For half an hour, the Allied center was given a respite; thirty precious minutes in which to strengthen and reorganize its attenuated line, to refresh its weary men. And in that half hour, command of the battlefield, the moral momentum so vital in battle, was restored to the Allies. Back beside the Duke, and still panting from his exertions, De Lancey said as much: "Napoleon has missed his chance!"

"Damn the fellow!" replied the Duke. "He is a mere pounder after all!"

Neither could know that the vital respite was due to the Emperor's failure to respond to Ney's desperate call for reinforcements to exploit his breakthrough. Napoleon had been unwilling to commit the fourteen battalions of the Guard, his finest troops, who were still held in reserve. Despite Ney's pleas and fulminations, the all-important moment had been allowed to pass, the British had been allowed to regroup, and already the French in La Haye Sainte were coming under heavy fire from British guns sited in commanding positions. Napoleon ordered a renewal of the cannonade, and his own guns opened fire on Wellington's center.

Once again the Duke passed the order for his troops to lie down where they were, and to endure yet another storm of shot and shell as best they might, but he himself, and perforce De Lancey also, remained mounted. Both of them realized that this furious bombardment could only presage yet another massive French attack, and this time everyone in the British lines knew who the attackers would be. Napoleon had kept his Imperial Guard, the cream of his army, aloof from the battle. Sooner or later, everyone knew, the Guard must come, and now the moment was at hand.

The Duke had been rejoined by staff officers returned from earlier missions, and now he and De Lancey were at the center of an animated group, all anxiously reviewing the Allied situation, and the likely direction of the Guard's expected attack. De Lancey was at Wellington's elbow, chatting with his Canadian cousin and staff captain, De Lancey Barclay, when both heard the Duke say with an anxiety rarely heard from him: "Night or the Prussians *must* come!" But whatever his inward misgivings, Wellington was quickly himself again. Impassive as ever, Wellington acknowledged a shot that whistled close by a startled Copenhagen with a terse: "Hard pounding, this, gentlemen!"

Seconds later it all came to an end for De Lancey. A French cannonball struck the ground directly behind his horse, ricocheted up, and struck him full in the back, between the shoulder blades. It pitched him forward clear out of his saddle and over his horse's head. He landed on his face thirty feet away, bounded to his feet with the reflex action of a strong young man, and then collapsed on his back in front of a horrified group of fellow officers.

Wellington was the first to dismount and come to his aid, followed by young Barclay. Together they raised De Lancey to a sitting position and undid his tight uniform collar. All the staff now dismounted and knelt around their wounded friend, regardless of the cannonade that still whistled about them.

Gripped by paralyzing pain in his whole upper body,

and knowing that his wound must be mortal, De Lancey was anxious not to distract the Duke and his staff at this crucial moment in the battle.

"Leave me, sir; leave me! I am done for!" he told the Duke and, when Barclay leaned over him, he said, in a lower tone of voice, "Pray tell them to leave me, and let me die in peace." But Wellington, anxious that his friend should not be accidentally run over and crushed by the artillery that was maneuvering nearby, or captured by a French foray, ordered him to be taken to the rear. Barclay had four soldiers spread a blanket on the ground onto which De Lancey was placed. With the assistance of another couple of soldiers from the nearest square, De Lancey was lifted and carried carefully back to the nearby farm of Mont St. Jean, where he was left in the lee of an outbuilding. Barclay knelt down by his stricken cousin for a last reassuring word. In a whisper now, for his strength was ebbing fast, De Lancey asked him to write to Magdalene at Antwerp. "Say everything kind, and break the news as gently as possible.

"And Barclay," he added, placing a hand on his friend's arm, "tell her that I send my dearest love and that my last thoughts are of her."

Barclay promised to write, if he should survive the battle, for no one could be sure of living through this terrible struggle in which it seemed everyone, on both sides, must be killed. After a last handclasp he stood up to leave. But a sudden flurry on the left, where a group of French skirmishers appeared unexpectedly on the crest of the ridge, made him uneasy about this exposed position. He had the little group of soldiers, still waiting nearby, take up their burden once again and carry De Lancey back to the little hamlet of Mont St. Jean. An open door gaped into a deserted barn, and it was into this shelter that De Lancey was borne. They left him lying as comfortably as possible on the hard earthen floor, and went back to the battle.

The Guard was coming! The word ran along the Allied line, soldier whispering it to soldier in a kind of awe and peering into the fog of gunsmoke that filled the valley for a glimpse of the Emperor's fabled Guardsmen, victors of a hundred battlefields and the most famous troops in the world. No one could see them at first, but, as the French batteries ceased their fire, they could be heard—the rum-a-tum-tum of the drums, the clash and clatter of their accoutrements, and, most fearsome of all, the hoarse shout from thousands of throats: "*Vive l'Empereur!*"

Suddenly they burst through the cloud that masked the valley floor, a wall of soldiers moving inexorably onward. Fifteen thousand men, grenadiers and chasseurs, led by Ney himself, hatless now and on foot, carrying in their packs the dress uniforms they would wear for the entry into Brussels, just as they had worn them for victory parades in every capital in Europe. The Allied guns opened fire on them, the balls plowing great gaps in the solid blocks of blue, but the gaps were filled as soon as they were made and the Guard came on at their majestic pace. Fifteen thousand bearded giants, their bearskin caps with the red plumes tossing above making them seem taller still, marched across the level ground and began the ascent. Their steady, disciplined tread seemed to shake the ground. Up the terrible blood-soaked slopes they came, marching over the dead and dying who covered the hillside, dividing into two imposing columns as they neared the top, one aimed at the Allied center, the other at the left flank.

And now the guns fell silent as the British gunners, after a last point-blank cannonade, abandoned their exposed batteries to find shelter among the infantry behind them. The French drums were deafening now, their rhythm quickening to the menacing *pas de charge*. The two columns, each one eighty men wide, topped the ridge, thousands of bayonets glittering waist high. With a last battle cry, "*L'Empereur!*" the Guard thrust forward with all their fabled élan.

Behind the Allied line all was silence. The British infantry lay in the trampled wheat until the French bearskins topped the skyline. A quiet word from Wellington alerted the commander of the British Guards regiments in his center: "Now, Maitland, now's your time!" A moment later, as the French drew within fifty yards, came the Duke's calm voice again: "Stand up, Guards!"

The eighty men leading the French column suddenly found themselves confronted by 1,500 red-coated British Guardsmen. At the sharp words of command, 1,500 muskets were leveled and aimed. "Make ready! Fire!"

The British fire shredded the oncoming French. As men fell, gaps appeared, but pressure from rear files forced the mass forward. A second volley crashed out, more devastating even than the first; the great column recoiled, came to a halt. A third volley ripped into the Guard, now mere lambs to the slaughter, and men at the flanks and the rear began to melt away from the column to avoid the fearful fire that awaited it at the top. The entire column, like some stricken animal, visibly wavered and then, slowly at first but with ever-quickening pace, began to retreat down the hill. For the first time in all its long, proud history, the Imperial French Guard acknowledged defeat, even—as more and more individuals broke rank to seek safety in the smoke-filled valley—rout. It was a terrible sight, for the Guard, in defeat as in victory, won awe from all who beheld it. There was a curious pause, a kind of communal gasp all along the Allied line, for on the far left Colborne's troops, led by his redoubtable 52nd Foot, had crumpled the French flanking column.

From the French side of the valley came the astounded, dismaying shout: "*La Garde recule!*" It was a cry of unbelief, of horror; a cry the Grande Armée had never heard before, and, as the shattered remnants of the Guard streamed back across the valley, the guns on both sides fell silent. Hougoumont smoldered and smoked, still held by its indomitable garrison; the grim British squares still clung to their ridgetop, the glittering masses of the French still covered the far slopes, yet on both sides there was a sudden awareness that the battle had reached its climax, the moment of decision.

Standing up in his stirrups on Copenhagen, beneath his elm tree, Wellington peered anxiously to his left, at the far right flank of the French. And there, surely, the twinkle of musketry; the Emperor's right flank was under assault. It could only be the Prussians! Blücher had arrived at last! Now, for the first time in all this long afternoon and evening, the Allies could go over to the offensive. Standing high in his stirrups, the Duke took off his hat and waved it three times.

It was a signal that everyone understood. All down the Allied line a great wave of cheering burst from thousands of parched throats. Men who had endured almost to the point of death forgot their exhaustion in the exhilaration of the moment and, with the smell of victory in their nostrils, surged forward to the attack, charging with leveled bayonets down the slope toward the silent French below.

The Duke galloped along the ridgetop, sending each regiment of his reserves, cavalry as well as infantry, forward in support of his first line, which was already heavily engaged. The assault was irresistible—the sheer momentum and excitement of the cheering British, Belgian, and Highland infantry swept all before them. Down their slope and across the valley floor the Allied line surged, the French retreating before them. But on the far side an unbroken French army awaited them. And then a curious thing happened. From a disengaged regiment in the Emperor's center there came a few cries, clearly heard by soldiers on both sides: "*Nous sommes trahis!*" We are betrayed!

In a matter of seconds the regiment broke formation, melting into a crowd of individuals seeking to escape. The panic spread like wildfire; in moments France's magnificent army, most of them veterans of a dozen campaigns, became a leaderless mob. The moral force that welds fearful individuals into a disciplined body, proud of its own prowess and contemptuous of danger, had suddenly snapped, leaving only a crowd of fear-crazed civilians struggling to escape British, Belgian, and Prussian bayonets. The panic was almost tangible, and no one was quicker to sense it than the Emperor himself at his command post at La Belle Alliance. At first he sought refuge within a square of the Guard, one of the four battalions still held in reserve, and in its safety he gained the road to the rear, where his carriage was waiting. This bore him from the field, but he was forced to leave its cushioned comfort at a block in the road and take to horseback, surrounded by a few staff officers with whom he rode hard for Paris. He had already sent a bulletin announcing his own decisive victory over Wellington, and he was anxious to reach his capital before the arrival of less pleasant news.

Behind him, the battle moved into its final stages, the last rays of the setting sun casting a red glow over a terrible scene. The valley was a sea of struggling men as the Allied cavalry, aided by Prussian hussars and lancers from Blücher's advancing army, hacked and hounded at the backs of the retreating French, now herded like sheep before them. Through this inchoate mob the four reserve battalions of the Guard moved like a ship through a stormy sea, marching with precision and aplomb in the wake of their fleeing Emperor, halting to fire a volley and present a bristling hedge of bayonets when pressed too close by swirling masses of Prussian cavalry, before resuming their march when the horsemen passed on to easier prey. Behind them Marshal Ney, blackened, burned, and bleeding, waved a broken sword and attempted to rally the panic-driven men streaming heedlessly past him.

"Come and see how a Marshal of France can die!" he challenged, but no one paid him any heed, save for a solitary corporal. Together these two fought their way across the field, through pursuers and pursued alike, until the darkness brought the fighting to an end. Together they limped over the hill towards the south, Ney the last French officer to leave the field.

In the gathering dusk Wellington rode slowly up the slope in the wake of the retreating French, and at La Belle Alliance he encountered Blücher in the center of a large staff. The two men, both of whom had placed their trust in the good faith of the other and had seen that trust splendidly vindicated, shook hands warmly. Blücher, horrified by the piles of dead all about them, gasped in his atrocious French: "*Quelle affaire!*" It was arranged that the Prussians should take up the pursuit, and Wellington returned to his own troops, who were now utterly spent.

To get his men free of the mounds of dead and dying that encumbered their former ridgetop position, he had them march clear of the field and bivouac for the night in the open, wherever they found themselves. His battle fought, his duty done, the Duke then betook himself to his quarters in the little inn at Waterloo, where he sat down at a large table set for all his staff. Impassive as ever, he ate in silence, looking up anxiously at the sound of any footstep outside in the hope that it might yet be one of his young officers still alive after the battle, but no one came.

It was after midnight and he had lain down on his pallet on the floor when his surgeon, John Hume, brought him the first casualty list, with the names of those officers already known to be dead and a rough estimate of the total dead and wounded. It was an appalling document, and, as he read slowly through it, the Duke's iron self-control cracked. He let the list fall and gazed vacantly about the room, and, as the significance of those empty chairs came home to him, he began, for the second time in his life, to weep before a horrified Hume.

One of those friends, whose empty chair he wept for, lay in a coma not far away. Colonel Sir William Howe De Lancey, quartermaster general, lay unnoticed in the darkness of an empty shed, his pain and misery merely a part of the communal agony of the stricken battlefield where, among the heaps of corpses, more than 40,000 men, Allied and French, lay wounded and helpless while 10,000 riderless horses, many of them horribly mangled, galloped in frenzy over the dead and dying. But a worse menace than trampling hooves were the looters, those dark forms already flitting about the field. They were Prussians and Belgians mostly—the British were too exhausted to stir beyond their bivouacs—and they moved silently among the piles of bodies, relieving officers of money and gold rings or watches, and other soldiers of any jewelry or prized possessions in their knapsacks. A wounded man opposing them would have his throat cut, and it was easiest to simply cut off any finger wearing a ring. The mouths of the dead were pried open and teeth smashed loose, for dentists anywhere would pay well for sound teeth that could be made up into dentures. The cries of their victims were lost in the dreadful outcry of thousands of dying men, some calling out for help, some on friends or loved ones, most simply moaning in their agony. The color, the cheering, the glory had left the battlefield, but the suffering, the killing, and the dying went on.

10
Odyssey

TRUE TO HER PROMISE, Magdalene De Lancey, after her husband's departure, had joined the swelling throng of English refugees, most of them women, streaming out of Brussels on the road to Antwerp and safety. She had not wanted to go; she would have preferred to stay as close to her husband as circumstances allowed. In Brussels, so close to the fighting, she could be sure of hearing quickly any news affecting him, whereas Antwerp, at a greater distance, was sure to mean delay. But she understood William's anxiety to leave her in a safe place, and unquestionably Brussels was too close to the battlefield—it could be overrun by a victorious French army, or swarms of Allied deserters, in a matter of hours.

Accordingly, after watching the last of the Allied regiments march out for Quatre Bras on Friday morning, she and Emma had taken their few pieces of luggage down to the carriage De Lancey had arranged for them, and made a slow journey to Antwerp on the coast, a few miles away. They were met on their arrival by a young Captain Mitchell, one of De Lancey's deputies, and escorted by him to a small inn, Le Grand Laboureur, located on a quiet back street in the central part of the town. Mistress and maid were installed in a sparsely furnished but adequate bedroom at the rear of the building, and here Captain Mitchell left them, after promising Magdalene to bring any news from the front as quickly as he could manage.

There was an air of excitement about Antwerp, a brisk and bourgeois sort of town, with none of the elegant airs and graces of the capital, Brussels. Its harbor, always busy, was now jammed with shipping, both naval and commercial, for many of the ships that had brought British troops, and not a few civilians, across to the Continent some days earlier were standing by in case an Allied reversal should require a British evacuation. The city itself was crowded with visitors of every sort, most of them with connections of some kind with Wellington's army, for it was from here that the army in the field was supplied and paid, and here that much of its administration was based. In addition to the traffic to and from Waterloo, a constant stream of wounded and sick soldiers, of messengers and officers on official business, passed through en route to London.

But whatever its intended functions, Antwerp's most thriving traffic was in news or, more usually, rumor. In a town where knowledge of what was going on somewhere else was all important, tongues wagged constantly, and each new arrival from London or, better still, from the front was sure of an eager audience. Human nature being what it is, bad news always took precedence over good. A dozen times the town quivered in delicious horror to tales of new disasters from the Allied front. The Duke had been utterly defeated at Quatre Bras; Blücher had been killed and his army was in full retreat for Prussia; Napoleon had crushed the Allied army, inflicting terrible losses, and the Grande Armée had entered Brussels in triumph. Such were but a few of the stories gleaned from refugees, deserters, and the wounded.

For Magdalene, conscious of her husband's responsibilities and anxious for his welfare, this avid and often malicious gossip was more than she could bear. In particular, she found the English women staying at her inn and billeted in houses nearby especially difficult to put up with. Most of them were, like her, wives of officers or officials in the town, and, having nothing better to occupy their time, they met daily to exchange rumors and surmises, usually of the wildest kind. They were all a good deal older than she and more experienced in the world of affairs, and consequently they treated her as a charming child. Presiding over these London expatriates was a Lady Hamilton, wife of a senior British official, who had taken it upon herself to be leader and spokeswoman for the English community in the town. To escape her patronage, Magdalene decided to stay in her room all day and have her meals sent up to her. She emerged only in the evening for a walk about the quieter streets of the town. It was the best way to ensure that she would receive any news of her husband directly, since he would send any message for her to the inn, and she would want to question any courier personally. In any event, she could be certain of learning all the gossip she could want, and more, through her maid. Emma was as avid for rumor as her mistress was uninterested in it; she spent every moment free from her duties out on the main streets of the city, where the sidewalks were abuzz with conversation.

Saturday, June 17, the day after Quatre Bras, had been particularly alarming. Hundreds of Belgian deserters had flocked into Antwerp, bringing with them wild tales of Allied disaster and French atrocities. Emma had been terrified by what she heard and, coming back to their room, had pleaded with Magdalene to take ship immediately, while they could, and wait in the security of England. The city was full of wounded soldiers and refugess, and all the English ladies from Brussels had embarked, she was sure, to escape the conquering French, who were already in Brussels; she implored her mistress to seek safety now, while they were still able.

Seeing that the girl was really frightened, Magdalene sat her down in a chair opposite hers and took both her hands to soothe her, while speaking as gently as possible.

"Now, Emma," she said, "you know that if the French were firing at this house I would not move till I was ordered, but you have no such duty. Therefore, go if you like; you have my permission, and I dare say any of these English families will let you join them. But I must stay."

Emma had broken down then and pressed her face, wet with tears, against Magdalene's hands. Between sobs she told her mistress that she would stay with her and never leave her, even if it meant going to a French prison.

Now, quite reconciled, the two women settled down to await events, but Emma still haunted the streets, anxious for news. For all her declared resolution, Magdalene found the waiting a sore trial. The sound of the guns at Quatre Bras had reached Antwerp, and she had closed the windows to shut out their rumble, but still it had persisted, like the muttering of distant thunder. She was dreadfully worried about her husband; they were both young and strong and, like all such young people, they expected that they would live forever, yet she had shared her husband's sudden intuitive premonition at the moment of parting, and now it left a doubt that gnawed at her heart. She knew that Wellington was notorious for exposing himself to enemy fire, and that her Will must be at his side. She yearned for word from him, the merest scribble to tell her that he was alive and well.

And, to her indescribable joy and relief, it arrived! Late on Saturday evening, the innkeeper's wife brought a note up to her; it had been brought to her, she said, by a soldier, only moments before. With pounding heart Magdalene opened the envelope, and there was the message, written in pencil in her husband's bold handwriting. They had beaten the French, he had written, but would have to do it again; for the rest, he was alive and well and in good spirits and sent his love. The scribbled endearments that ended his note brought a happy glow to her cheeks.

Later that same Saturday night, Captain Mitchell himself arrived full of news. Wellington had beaten Ney at Quatre Bras the day before, he confirmed, but the Prussians had not fared so well at Ligny. There were confused reports of the fighting there, and even a rumor that Blücher himself had been killed, but in any event they were falling back to regroup and, accordingly, Wellington's army was pulling back also. The main Allied effort would be made tomorrow, Sunday, and it would likely be a very great battle indeed, to be fought somewhere just a little south of Brussels itself, probably near the village of Waterloo.

Captain Mitchell was full of good advice also. He warned Magdalene to keep off the streets as much as possible; the town was full of deserters and walking wounded after the battle at Quatre Bras, and there seemed to be too many French sympathizers among the local populace for comfort. She should keep her bags packed and be ready to move at a moment's notice. If tomorrow's battle should go badly, she and all the remaining English women would have to be evacuated promptly in order to clear the port for the possible embarkation of Wellington's troops. But he, too, had had a communication from Colonel De Lancey, and he could assure her that her husband had come through the battle unscathed and was his usual confident, clear-thinking self. Captain Mitchell was a nice young man who obviously idolized her husband, and Magdalene's heart warmed to him. She thanked him for all his kindnesses to Emma and herself, assured him that she would follow his instructions and heed his warnings, and sent him on his way loaded with thanks and compliments.

She slept well that night, her mind at ease for once with the knowledge that her husband was safe and sound, and next morning she wrote him another letter. Every day she planned to write him, as promised, to ease the pain of separation. Half the letter was a chronicle of her days' happenings and assurances as to the health and comfort of Emma and herself, but in the second half there was room only for love. She told him how keenly she missed him, and poured out her heart in a torrent of endearments.

She sealed the letter and sent it on its way to Captain Mitchell for forwarding to the front. She felt better once she had sent it and somehow closer to her beloved husband; she was not to know that De Lancey never received any of her notes. But at noon her apprehensions returned, her spirits sank. From far to the south came the sound of gunfire, and gunfire, moreover, such as she had never heard before. A great battle was raging there, the cannonading became ever more furious. She could stand it no longer; she closed the windows of her room to shut out the sound, but the thunder grew worse, so intense that the very windows shook. She closed her eyes and pressed her fingers to her ears and tried to blot out both the sound and the very thought of those frightful guns.

She was not alone in her fears; even the old soldiers in the town, veterans of many a battle, looked apprehensively to the south and muttered among themselves. On the Kentish shores of England, 135 miles away, villagers heard the distant rumble of the guns and wondered. No one had ever heard anything like it before.

All day the thunder waxed and waned, building to a fearful climax just before dusk and then finally falling away altogether as darkness descended. Magdalene had been very nervous during the cannonade but when it fell silent she knew real fear, for with silence had come the realization that the fighting was over, the battle lost or won. The firing had been so long, so intense—could her husband have survived it? Was he lying dead or possibly, even at this very moment, dreadfully wounded somewhere on that distant field, in desperate need of help, and she so far away and helpless to assist?

But Magdalene was a sensible young woman of strong character, and knew she must accept whatever fate had decided to send her way. Being young, and therefore a natural optimist, she assured herself that De Lancey had survived the battle, as he had so many others, and composed herself to sit down and write her daily letter to her husband. She told him of her foolish fears and ended with her feelings of relief, now that the dreadful battle was over and she could look forward to being with him again in a day or so.

She felt much better when she had finished writing. Setting out her fears had helped her to rid herself of them, and, as her anxiety faded, so her eagerness grew to see her beloved, to run into his arms and hold him close. Emma had returned as the evening drew on, and the two waited together, in a fever of impatience, drinking cups of tea and talking in subdued voices, as if afraid of missing something important, some step upon the stair perhaps. At midnight they went to bed. Emma fell asleep instantly, but Magdalene, lying fully dressed on her bed in case she had to get up quickly, could only toss and turn. Towards dawn, however, her tired mind gave way, and she fell into an exhausted slumber.

The cheerful rattling of dishes awoke them on Monday morning. The innkeeper's wife bustled in with a breakfast tray, and the smell of coffee and brioches dispelled any lingering doubts and fears of the night before. And hard on the heels of breakfast came Captain Mitchell. Magdalene knew a moment of real fear when she heard his jingling step upon the stair, but when the door was opened to reveal his cheerful, smiling face she experienced a sense of relief so profound that she nearly fainted. So bright-faced a messenger could only be the bearer of good news, and so it proved. Wellington had won a great victory after a tremendous battle, he told them; furthermore, he had seen the first list of casualties, showing all the senior officers killed yesterday, and De Lancey's name was not on it! He must be alive and well. Magdalene's joy and relief were so great that she burst into tears and found herself both laughing and sobbing as she poured out her thanks to a gratified Captain Mitchell.

She was sure now that there would be a message for her from her husband soon, and she waited in her room in a fever of expectation, but the message, when it came, was from a quite unexpected source. Lady Hamilton sent to invite her to visit her for a few moments in her house nearby. It was a very unusual invitation, at a very unusual time of day, but in her happiness Magdalene was prepared to indulge everyone, and especially a woman who, she was sure, felt kindly toward her, even though Magdalene found it difficult to like her.

Whirled along in her own cloud of happiness, she made her way to the Hamilton house, and found herself in the midst of a number of ladies, all of whom looked very grave and somber indeed. Many of them, like Lady Hamilton herself, had managed to attach themselves in some capacity or other to British headquarters there, and so would be concerned with all manner of sad news from so terrible a battlefield; few of them, Magdalene realized, could have been the recipients of such wonderful news as she had received, and she felt a guilty pang of remorse.

"I am so sorry," she apologized, and assumed a thoughtful and concerned expression, more in keeping with the atmosphere of the room.

"Come here, child, and sit by me," commanded Lady Hamilton in an unusually gentle voice. "I have something of the gravest importance to tell you."

Pierced now by deep misgiving, Magdalene did so. Lady Hamilton took one of Magdalene's hands in hers, as one might soothe a fractious child, and, while the other ladies in the room looked on with silent sympathy, she told her what she had done. She had been at headquarters, she said, when the first list of casualties had come in from Waterloo. Sir William's name had been on it, but she had removed it in order to break the news more gently and personally to Magdalene. She felt this to be her duty as a friend, she explained. Magdalene must now brace herself for a shock. Her husband was desperately wounded; his name had been one of the first to be listed in the report of casualties among Wellington's senior officers.

Magdalene was never to remember just what happened after that. The shock of the truth, after such euphoria, seemed to numb all her faculties, reducing the world about her to the quality of a dream. In a sort of blur she managed to take her leave of Lady Hamilton and her assembled friends and make her way back to her room, walking past Emma with sightless eyes and throwing herself full-length upon her bed. It was not grief or mere sorrow she felt— her eyes were dry—so much as shock, disbelief, and a sort of confused anger.

But common sense quickly restored itself, and with it came an instant perception of where her duty lay. Her husband was lying somewhere, dreadfully wounded; she must make her way to Waterloo, find him, and do everything she could for him. Promptly, but calmly, she sent for the innkeeper and ordered a carriage, impressing him with the need for the greatest urgency and speed. Then she explained the situation to Emma and with her set about the task of packing the few necessities they would need for the trip. Each minute, she was aware, could mean the difference between seeing her husband alive or dead.

The carriage was brought in a remarkably short time; the inn's hostler himself acted as coachman. The two women bundled themselves into its stuffy interior, and they were off, rattling over the cobblestones on the road to Brussels.

The highway to the capital, when they reached it, was almost impassable, choked with carts and carriages of every sort, all heading toward Antwerp. They filled the road, making progress towards Brussels all but impossible, and traffic jams were frequent as cursing, whip-wielding drivers fought to disentangle their vehicles. And as their carriage slowly picked its way through the confused masses of angry men and weary horses, they found themselves stemming a stream of another sort: a positive river of soldiers on foot, walking wounded or deserters, all straggling away from the battlefield and anxious to reach the safety of Antwerp and its port. The wounded, bandaged and bloodstained and gray-faced with weariness, presented no problem to the travelers, apart from the slow task of forcing a way through them, but the deserters, mostly Belgians desperate with the knowledge of their grievous offense in running away, were another matter. Many were carrying clothing and household effects, obviously looted from houses along their route, and these lawless bands represented a real threat to two helpless women caught in their midst. Magdalene pulled up the shutters on the carriage; it made the interior dark and airless, but she felt safer away from the bold, inquiring eyes of these ruffians.

Magdalene was in a fever to reach her husband, and the constant delays were an agony for her. She felt that if she could find him alive, to share only five minutes with him, she would cheerfully give up her own life, and she could not bear the thought that his life might be ebbing away while she was caught in a jumble of horses and men on the Brussels road, unable to reach him in time. Their hostler-coachman was doing his best, she knew, but progress was painfully slow, and growing worse as they left Antwerp behind.

It was while they were stopped, waiting for a tangle of carts, loaded with wounded, to sort themselves out, that Magdalene, peering out between the shutters, caught sight of a familiar face in the stream of pedestrians passing by. It was Captain William Hay, an officer of the 16th Light Dragoons, one of De Lancey's old regiments. De Lancey and he had served together and become friends years ago, and Magdalene had met him on various social occasions since. Here was a priceless opportuntity to ask for news of her husband. Magdalene lowered the shutter and called out to him. He turned about when he heard his name, caught sight of her, and made his way over to the carriage. It was only then that Magdalene noticed his bandaged right arm, and her first inquiry was about the nature of his wound, and whether she could do anything to be of help. Captain Hay told her his arm had been hit by a musket ball, but not seriously. The surgeons had attended to it and put him on a cart bound for Antwerp. He had simply gotten off to stretch his legs while the cart got itself clear of a traffic tangle, and he was with friends and well looked after.

Despite his assurances, his face wore a very grave and serious aspect, most unlike his usual lively manner, and he now asked Magdalene what had brought her out on this dangerous road. She told him she was trying to find her husband, lying wounded somewhere near Waterloo, and now Captain Hay looked very solemn indeed.

"Do you know anything?" she asked.

"I fear I have bad news for you," he replied, and then, after a pause in which Magdalene held her breath, he told her he had heard, from an officer who had been present, that De Lancey had been killed by a cannonball at Wellington's side, and Hay himself had seen the Duke's dispatch in which he listed De Lancey as killed.

"I'm afraid there can be no doubt, ma'am," Hay concluded. "Your husband is dead, and probably already buried."

It was a stunning blow. For a moment Magdalene's mind ceased working and she sat staring before her with sightless eyes, incapable of any sort of thought. Painfully aware of the effect of his message, Hay moved away from the carriage and was soon lost from sight in the crowd of refugees. It was not until Emma, anxiously clutching her elbow, managed to gain her attention that Magdalene was again conscious of the world about her.

"Surely we had better go back now, ma'am," Emma was urging, and as Magdalene became aware of her worried face and that of the coachman at the window, she made an effort to force her mind, numbed with shock, to cope with the problems of the present.

"Yes, yes!" she assented, and then closed her eyes as a wave of pain engulfed her. He was dead! Her husband, her Will, her dear lover who was her whole life, was gone forever. She could not believe it, could not accept it, could not bear even to begin to contemplate life without him. In a nightmare of agonized distraction Magdalene was borne back to Antwerp, sitting upright with her eyes tightly closed while her maid watched her anxiously.

It was an easier passage for the coach this time, heading in the same direction as everyone else on the road, but Magdalene was quite unconscious of it. Emma led her upstairs on arrival at the inn, shaking her head at the proffered assistance of a concerned innkeeper, and helped Magdalene to her bed. She left her then, stretched out with a cool, damp cloth covering her eyes, and, after drawing the curtains to shut out the bright sunlight, she quietly withdrew, leaving her mistress alone with her grief.

Early in the evening Emma came upstairs again with a tray. Magdalene wanted no food, but Emma persuaded her to take some soup, and afterward she helped her mistress prepare for bed, speaking as little as possible in deference to her obviously distracted state of mind. As she left, Magdalene told her she did not wish to be disturbed, and Emma heard the key turn in the lock as she went downstairs.

That night Magdalene tortured herself with the thoughts of what might have been. If only she had been able to share a little more time with her husband, now that she realized how precious each moment was; if she could have had just five minutes with him, alive and conscious, she felt that she would ask no more of life. It was now, too, that realization came to her of the full extent of Lady Hamilton's mistaken kindness. For Lady Hamilton, by her own admission, had seen Wellington's first list of casualties and De Lancey had been shown there, according to Captain Hay, as killed, not merely badly wounded, as Lady Hamilton had told her. That wild trip, with its vain hopes and shattering revelation, had been the result of a well-meant but foolish attempt to spare her feelings, to break the bad news in degrees, rather than to tell it to her all at once. They had meant to be kind, Lady Hamilton and her friends, but they had been cruel beyond their imaginings.

She slept fitfully. Between periods of grief and agony almost beyond endurance, physical exhaustion asserted itself, and she fell into troubled slumber. Shortly after dawn she was wakened by someone tapping at her door, one of Lady Hamilton's friends no doubt, but she was in no mood for formal condolences, however well meant, and she called out as politely as she could that she wanted to be left alone. The footsteps retreated, and she was left to herself in the semi-darkness.

It seemed only minutes later that she heard a familiar

step on the stair, a perfunctory rap on the door, and a familiar voice calling to her. It was Emma, and she would not go away, even though Magdalene had called out that she did not need her, that she would be quite all right if she could just be left alone for a little peace. Emma insisted she had urgent news for her, news from Captain Mitchell. At the mention of that officer's name, Magdalene reluctantly got up and unlocked the door to an excited Emma.

"He's alive, ma'am, he's alive!" she exclaimed, almost beside herself with delight and excitement, and it took some moments before Magdalene could calm her sufficiently to give an intelligible account of the message that Captain Mitchell had entrusted to her.

A staff officer, poking about the deserted village of Mont St. Jean, had found a wounded officer lying on the floor of a cowshed. He was badly hurt but conscious and had asked that a message be sent to his wife, Lady De Lancey, at Le Grand Laboureur, Antwerp. The staff officer had reported his find to his superior, Sir George Scovell, the commandant for the area, and a surgeon had been sent to attend the wounded man. The surgeon had bled him twice and held out hope for his recovery, the message noted, and Captain Mitchell had taken it upon himself to arrange for a carriage and a driver to be at Lady De Lancey's disposal in an hour's time.

Magdalene was overwhelmed by the news. To have hoped, only to have those hopes cruelly shattered, and then to hope again was almost more than she could bear. And yet she trusted Captain Mitchell, knew him to be a friend and hardly the man to pass on baseless rumor. Captain Hay could have been mistaken; he had, after all, been reporting what he had heard, what he had read, not what he had himself witnessed.

In any event, there was no doubt about going. Any chance to see her husband, however insubstantial, must be seized upon, and she and Emma were soon seated in a carriage and making their way yet again down that frightful road to Brussels. The traffic this morning was, if anything, even worse than on the previous day. In addition to the carts and strays and walking wounded of yesterday there were now detachments of Allied troops, light cavalry mostly, bound somewhere on official business and impatient of delay, like cavalrymen everywhere. Beyond Brussels the road became almost impassable, jammed with soldiers and civilians alike, as well as carts and horses and even, in one place, a battery of horse artillery, their gunners, frustrated and furious, using language that made Emma stop up her ears and that Magdalene could barely recognize as English. Through all this their coachman battled bravely, traveling mostly on the shoulder of the crowded road and occasionally, when the ground was firm enough, even cutting across roadside fields to escape some traffic tangle.

As they neared Waterloo and turned down the road to the battlefield itself, there was more than mere traffic to cope with. The roadside was increasingly littered with dead horses and even, here and there, with dead men. The air grew heavy with the stink of corruption. At one pile of corpses the horses screamed at the smell of death, shying away and rearing so violently that it was all that the coachman could do to keep them from bolting. At a tiny crossroads hamlet there was even worse to come. Army surgeons had set up shop in one of the buildings and outside there was a large pile of human legs and arms, limbs amputated from wounded soldiers and tossed outside until they could be disposed of. Nearby, on the verge of the road, more wounded men lay, awaiting the moment when they would be carried in, placed on a rough kitchen table, given a roll of tough leather to bite on, and held down by brawny assistants while the surgeon sliced off a smashed limb or probed for and cut out a musket ball.

They bore the wait with surprising fortitude, smoking or drinking rum supplied by the surgeon's helpers. Some were chatting, others lay still, and a few were obviously already dead, but there was a certain calmness to the scene: it seemed to be a comfort to die, as one had lived, in ordered ranks, shoulder to shoulder with one's comrades.

To Magdalene the sight of so much death and pain— the long lines of mangled men, the piles of amputated limbs, the heaps of dead—was appalling. She gazed about, wide-eyed with horror, as the frightened horses found their way through the cluttered hamlet and out onto the ridge beyond, where, for the first time, Magdalene had a glimpse of the battlefield itself. The driver, unwilling to go further across this terrible space and uncertain of which way to turn, drew rein, and the little party looked about in silence while the horses rolled their eyes with fright, shaking foam-flecked heads and stamping with impatience to be quit of this fearful place.

Directly below and in front lay the remains of a British infantry square, scattered lines of red-coated corpses surrounded on three sides by a pile of men and horses five feet high, and a tumbled mass of helmets, swords, and carbines. A gun, a British six-pounder with a broken trail and one wheel missing, lay canted at a crazy angle nearby, and the slopes beyond and the hillside opposite were carpeted with trampled grain and the bodies of men and horses. The carnage defied belief; Magdalene could scarcely credit that the thick drifts and piles that covered the ground as far as the eye could see were of dead men, but the stink of corruption told her otherwise. These corpses had been lying under a hot sun for two days, and the bodies of the horses were already bloated grotesquely. Here and there movement showed that the living were at work here too—there were little parties of men turning over bodies on the slopes, searching for anyone with the breath of life still in them, and hundreds of riderless horses moved about the far hillside, peacefully cropping the ground among the corpses.

Not a word was spoken. Emma sat frozen with fright opposite her mistress as the coachman wheeled his terrified charges about and made his way back to ask directions. Outside the surgery they had passed earlier, Magdalene recognized an officer chatting with some of the wounded; it was Lieutenant-General John MacKenzie, an old friend of De Lancey's, whom she had met in Brussels, and she called out to him as the coachman drew rein: "Can you tell me anything about my husband?"

"Why, I can tell you that he's alive!" MacKenzie responded heartily, and then, seeing Magdalene's obvious agitation, he pointed down the street and gave them directions as to exactly where De Lancey was to be found.

"I left him not five minutes since. He was in good form, and a surgeon was busy with him, applying leeches," he added with a wave as the carriage set off. Following his instructions, it drew up outside the open front of a sort of lean-to shed next to a plaster-fronted peasant's cottage. Breathless with excitement, her heart pounding with mingled fear and hope, Magdalene descended from the carriage and, going over to the door, peered into the musty darkness within, almost dreading what she might find.

Inside, a huddled form lay on a scattering of straw on the earthen floor. It turned its head as she entered and she saw again that familiar face, pale now and unshaven, but dearer to her than all the world.

She had found her husband, and she threw herself on her knees beside him to smother him in kisses and tears of joy.

11

Honeymoon Cottage

THAT FIRST DAY together had for Magdalene the quality of a dream in which unlikely people drifted in and out of impossible situations, events transpired without logical sequence, and laughter mingled with tears, happiness with sadness. Surely only in a dream could she find herself kneeling on an earthen floor, overcome with joy to find her gravely wounded husband. Only in a dream, surely, would her husband, a brilliant soldier and a Knight of the Bath, be holding court lying on a bundle of dirty straw. Only in a dream would so many exalted personages be crowding into a filthy cowshed to exchange compliments and cheerful badinage with her shattered husband and herself.

And yet it had all happened just so. After the first rapture of reunion, the kisses, the tears of happiness, had come the realization that De Lancey was, indeed, terribly wounded, his whole physical aspect subtly changed. It was not merely his pallor, or the unaccustomed shadow of his unshaven growth of beard, but rather the anguish in his eyes, the strained quality of even his smile and his laughter. For there had been both smiles and laughter in those first moments together, and in the crowded hours that followed; a day in which she had glowed with pride while her husband was praised and complimented by a succession of illustrious visitors.

De Lancey had told her about the circumstances in which he had been hit, although he was more concerned to tell her something of the battle itself. The spell of that long ordeal and its seemingly endless slaughter still had him in its grip, in a sort of feverish excitement that made it difficult for him to talk about anything else. His injury, he assured her, was no great matter; something was broken inside his upper abdomen so that it was painful sometimes to take a breath, but he was sure it would come out right in the end. He had feared at first that the wound was mortal, so great had been the shock and so intense the pain, but there was no external laceration and he merely needed to rest. So he said, at any rate, but his assurances lacked conviction; Magdalene was shocked by his pallor and his weakness, which left him exhausted after their animated conversation.

She asked him to lie still and rest while she told him of her own doings, but she was interrupted by the return of the surgeon who had been attending him and who had just had word of her arrival. He introduced himself as Surgeon Powell and explained to her that he believed that De Lancey had just missed being struck by the cannonball itself, but so narrowly that the wind of the shot, the blast in other words, had hit him with such terrible force that he had been knocked from his horse and had suffered some as yet undetermined internal injury.

Emma and the coachman, who had been hanging back at the entrance to the shed with what deference they could muster, to give their mistress a few moments of privacy with her husband, drew nearer to catch the surgeon's words as he explained De Lancey's injury, so that there was a considerable audience that looked on, in awed silence, as the patient was gently turned over so that his back, bruised but with the skin unbroken, could be properly exhibited. In a case like this, the surgeon explained, the best treatment was to draw off blood, to encourage the body to make more healthy blood and so stimulate the healing process. He had already bled De Lancey twice and would visit him again tomorrow to bleed him further, and in the meantime he recommended that leeches be placed near the heart to maintain the process.

"Will you show me how it's done?" Magdalene asked. "I shall be looking after him myself, and I should like to do everything I can to relieve the burden on you, for I know how busy you must be just now."

She watched with horrified fascination as Powell lifted one of the wriggling little creatures, hardly the size of a fingernail, from its container and placed it on her husband's chest. It instantly attached itself firmly to the skin and immediately began to swell and darken until, bloated with blood, it could be removed and placed back in the box with its fellows. Her own flesh tingled with revulsion and her gorge rose as she grasped one of these odious little monsters in the tweezers Powell provided, but she overcame her feelings and was able to carry out the operation to the surgeon's satisfaction.

"We shall make a first-class nurse of you in no time!" he declared, and explained to her what had to be done to keep her patient comfortable and to ease the strain on his breathing as much as possible. Powell left then; he had his hands full with operations waiting to be done at the makeshift surgery down the road, and dozens of patients recovering from wounds of every sort, but he promised Magdalene that he would look in on De Lancey each day, whenever he could manage. The coachman had departed, too; Magdalene had dispatched him back to Antwerp once it was clear that De Lancey was in no state to be moved. She was concerned now with finding a proper bed for her husband under better shelter than a leaky cowshed could provide. She sent Emma out to scout about the cottages nearby, to see whether there might be a suitable one still empty into which they might move their patient. She was determined not to leave her husband lying on an earth floor with nothing but a few handfuls of straw and his coat to ease his discomfort and a big, dilapidated door letting in the cold night air.

She had no sooner sent Emma about her mission than there was a great clatter of hooves outside, and Magdalene looked out to see what the commotion was about. An open two-wheeled curricle, all shining black paint and glittering brass and drawn by two smart black horses, had pulled up outside the door. Getting out of it and coming toward her was none other than the great Duke himself, accompanied by another officer whom Magdalene did not recognize. Wellington greeted her warmly; he had great affection for her and always treated her with the utmost gallantry. He introduced his companion as his aide-de-camp, Colonel Felton Hervey. They had been on the point of leaving to rejoin the army at Nivelles, the Duke explained, when word had come that De Lancey was alive, and they had come at once to see him.

"How is he? How is he?" Wellington asked, but before Magdalene could reply he had turned to Hervey and exclaimed: "Poor fellow! Poor fellow! We have been friends for years; I have known him since he was a boy."

Without a word, Magdalene led them inside, where the Duke immediately knelt down beside an obviously delighted De Lancey.

"My dear fellow! How are you, eh? How are you?" he asked, taking De Lancey's hand in his.

"Well enough, sir, I thank you," De Lancey replied, and then, in response to the Duke's questions, he described what had happened to him since he had been struck from his horse and carried from the field.

"Well, well, we thought you were dead, and I put you

down as killed on my casualty list," Wellington exclaimed. "Why, De Lancey, you will have the advantage of Sir Condy in *Castle Rackrent*: you will know what your friends said of you after you were dead!"

De Lancey smiled at his reference to a stage farce they had seen together and responded: "I hope I shall."

The Duke stood up to leave then, telling De Lancey that he would be sending his personal surgeon, John Hume, to attend him and to see that he recovered as quickly as possible.

"You must be with us when we reach Paris!" he added, as he took his leave.

Outside he told Magdalene that he had asked his area commander, Sir George Scovell, to do everything possible to be of assistance to her and her patient, and that Hume would be in regular attendance. As he turned to leave, his attention was caught by a cartload of wounded soldiers making its way down the street, and he watched it gravely until it drew up outside the surgery.

"I never want to fight another such battle!" he told Magdalene in a low voice. "It has been too much to see such brave men, so equally matched, cutting each other to pieces."

He rode off with Hervey, and Magdalene watched the curricle making its way down the cluttered street, a little knot of wounded soldiers at the corner raising a thin cheer as they recognized the distinctive features of its principal occupant, before she turned back to her patient.

Emma returned, but her reconnaissance had turned up nothing. However, she had established that the cottages in the immediate vicinity had been reoccupied, their owners having returned once it was clear that the menace of the French had been removed once and for all.

She told De Lancey what she had in mind; he was in great spirits after the flattering attentions of his commander-in-chief, and seemed to have regained something of his old animation and color. Magdalene left him in Emma's care and went back out into the street.

There did not seem to be much to choose from. Two rows of plaster-fronted peasant cottages, shabby and unpainted, faced one another across the rutted roadway, each narrow building much like the others. She decided to try the nearest first and rapped on the door of the cottage next to the cowshed. The owner, when he appeared, was an elderly farmer and, in her schoolgirl French, Magdalene explained to him what she was looking for. Could she rent a room in his cottage for her wounded husband? she asked. She would be willing to pay well and wanted only a warm bed and a good roof to keep her patient comfortable. The peasant, it appeared—Magdalene had trouble understanding his speech, so different from the Parisian French she had been taught—was a widower, living alone, and he seemed amenable to the idea. He took most of his meals with his son and daughter-in-law who lived just across the street, and he could move in with them for a time to be of assistance to the wounded English milord, always providing that the price was right.

Magdalene struck a deal with him there and then; the sum was, of course, far too generous, she was sure, judging by the alacrity with which her offer was accepted, but she was in no position to bargain and anxious only to get her husband settled as quickly as possible. But her heart sank when the peasant led her into his cottage and she had her first look at the interior.

It was indescribably dirty, filled with the squalid clutter of an old man living by himself. The stone-paved floor was covered with dirt tracked in by muddy boots over the years, and the small, solitary window was almost obscured by cobwebs. But behind the dirt and disarray, Magdalene could see that the essentials were there—a solid, if narrow, bed built into one corner, a table with three chairs, and a ladder-like stair leading to a sort of loft, with another cot and stool there providing additional sleeping-space. There were adequate dishes and pots, mostly unwashed, and a wide hearth for cooking. The stone-built privy out behind was an absolute horror, but its owner showed it off with some pride and obviously considered it a desirable amenity, if not a luxury, and Magdalene did her best to hide her revulsion.

In a matter of moments the deal was done; Magdalene handed over the agreed sum, and the farmer gathered up a few garments and departed, leaving her in sole possession. She put a brave face on her misgivings and returned to her invalid charge next door.

She found him holding court again. This time his visitor was a short, ruddy-faced officer who introduced himself as Sir Francis Dundas, an old Peninsular War crony of De Lancey's who, passing through Waterloo en route to join the army at Nivelles, had heard of De Lancey's miraculous delivery from the dead, as he laughingly called it, and had interrupted his journey to come and congratulate his old friend on his survival. He was very pleasant company indeed, and both Magdalene and De Lancey enjoyed his cheerful chatter and were sorry when he began to take his departure. Standing at the door with him, Magdalene explained their plans to move into the nearby cottage; her first concern, she went on, would be to provide some clean blankets for her patient, as she could not bring herself to entrust him to the dirty bedding in the house, which she was sure was verminous.

"What, no blankets?" exclaimed Dundas. "Why, I have one right here on my horse; no soldier moves a step without one. Allow me to make you a present of it—I shall have no trouble replacing it."

He unstrapped it from the roll behind his saddle and

left it with her, saluting gallantly as he rode off, and Magdalene turned to the task of moving her husband into his new quarters.

Emma proved an invaluable assistant. Between them they stripped the bed and put the cottage in some sort of order; a proper housecleaning was needed but would have to wait. Emma was able to fetch a couple of orderlies from the makeshift surgery down the street, and with their help De Lancey was gently eased off the ground where he had lain ever since the battle two days before, and borne on a stretcher into the cottage. A reasonably comfortable bed was contrived with Dundas's blanket and an array of greatcoats. Magdalene's own coat of soft, smooth material was rolled into a passable pillow. In a very short time De Lancey was established in some sort of comfort, in a proper bed under a dry roof and with a loving wife and her maid in attendance. He was able to smile and congratulate her on her achievement.

"And now you have an invalid husband on your hands," he said. "Are you a good nurse?"

"I have not been much tried," she replied with an answering smile, kneeling beside his bed. "But I am sure I shall learn, if you will be patient with me."

"Ah, my dear," he replied, "it is only fair to warn you I am likely to prove a difficult patient. I cannot bear the thought of lying idle here on my backside while you wait on me night and day."

Yet, for all their misgivings, their first night together since their separation in Brussels, which seemed ages ago, was supremely happy. Each was aware of the miracle that had brought them together again, enjoying life after having feared death. While Emma slept soundly on her cot in the loft, the two lovers kept as close as possible all night long. Magdalene slept fitfully on a makeshift pallet on the floor beside her husband, holding his hand in hers when he awoke, and soothing him when the pain of his wound made him restless and fretful. And for all its broken slumber, its squalor and discomfort, their first night together in this ramshackle peasant's hovel was, for both of them, a sort of idyll.

Wednesday morning brought another visitor. "Mr. John R. Hume, at your service, ma'am," he introduced himself when Magdalene answered the knock on their door. He was a large, hearty fellow, loud of voice and bluff of manner, but, for all his air of cheerful confidence, Magdalene distrusted his watery eye and flushed face and noticed the smell of gin that enveloped him. The personal surgeon to the Duke of Wellington was a skilled butcher who was reputed to have amputated more limbs than any man in the history of British medicine, but as she watched him make his examination of De Lancey, Magdalene's heart sank. He was obviously nonplussed by the absence of any open wound and, as he rattled on in his loud, assertive voice about the peculiar manifestations of fright and shock and trauma, she began to sense that any sort of internal injury, anything beyond mangled limbs and gunshot wounds, was quite beyond the realm of his expertise. He was making De Lancey angry with his jocular banterings about shamming injuries, and his examination was obviously causing intense pain. Once, when he was forced to sit erect, De Lancey nearly fainted with agony, and several times he bit his lip to prevent crying out as Hume probed and prodded his upper torso.

In the end Hume recommended the treatment as before, and bled De Lancey with the deftness of long experience; her poor husband was so pale already, Magdalene wondered if these surgeons would bleed him dry. Throughout his stay Hume made it clear, by his words and manner, that he was here at the express command of the commander-in-chief, taken away from more pressing cases to indulge a relatively healthy patient who happened to be a friend of the Duke. Magdalene neither liked nor trusted him, and she could see that he was actually harming her husband, so, as she saw him off at the door, she urged him not to interrupt his urgent practice any further. She would care for her husband with the assistance of the regular army surgeons nearby, and she would get in touch with him if the condition of the patient deteriorated. Hume seemed pleased to assent and made his departure with the air of a man happy to be relieved of an onerous burden. For his part, De Lancey seemed content to see him go, and listened with a rueful smile as Magdalene told him what she had done.

"Mind you, he's quite right, you know," he admonished her. "He's got far better things to do with his time than mucking about with me, with half the British army to attend to!"

Magdalene now set about her own program of nursing. She had managed to clean and open the cottage's one window the previous night, and she set Emma to sweeping up the disgraceful floor and washing the rest of the pots and bowls, while she herself attended to the patient. She fed him the soup she made from the meager food available, the soldier's field rations of dried peas and jerked beef being too coarse for De Lancey to swallow unless reduced to liquid form. He was her husband, not her baby, he protested, but Magdalene insisted on feeding him herself, a spoonful at a time, after she noticed that he grimaced with pain each time he tried to raise the spoon to his lips. Whatever it was, his injury affected only the upper part of his body, and any movement there, even that involved in breathing, had to be undertaken with great care.

Once she had fed him, Magdalene set about making her patient presentable. She brought him soap and water to wash his hands and then, at his directions, fetched his razor from the case he always carried at his belt. With infinite slowness, infinite care, she then shaved him, a process accompanied by much eye-rolling and silent appeals by the patient and suppressed breath, muttered exclamations, and relieved gasps on the part of the barber. And when she had finished, had washed and towelled the last trace of soap from his face, and saw again her handsome husband, free of grime and beard, she was so delighted with her work that she kissed him again and again, while they both laughed with delight at what they had accomplished.

She fetched his comb then, and set about the surprisingly difficult task of arranging his hair. When she parted it on the wrong side at first, De Lancey did not utter a word to set her right, but looked reproachfully at her when she stood back to inspect her work. She burst out laughing at how odd he looked, so very different from his normal appearance, but before he could make further protest she resumed her efforts and soon got it more or less right. She held a mirror for him then, and they both exclaimed with pleasure at her success.

Thus, their second caller of the day found them in good heart, the patient cheerful, the nurse confident, and the cottage swept and in good order. Sir George Scovell, a kindly, gentle-mannered man, a gray-haired soldier of the old school, with courtly manners and a limp acquired in some long-ago action, was the area commander, with a thousand responsibilities, most of them pressing, but he apologized to De Lancey for not having called on him earlier. When the army had moved on, he had been left with the tag ends of a campaign and a battle to look after: thousands of wounded to attend to, deserters to round up, looters to punish, convalescents and drafts of recruits to be sent on to their regiments, and rations to be found and distributed in an area desperately short of food. There was not an egg or a chicken, a pig or a sheep, to be found in the whole of the countryside, he declared, and most of the crops had been trampled flat by the maneuverings of two great armies and the foraging of thousands upon thousands of hungry soldiers. But he insisted that the

De Lanceys consider themselves his guests, free to call upon him for whatever they might require and his limited means could supply. He would try to send what food was available, he promised, although it might be only a turnip or two and some bread from the village bakery, which he was hoping to have operating again shortly, the baker having just returned home. And he would send some better bedding for the patient, he told Magdalene, with a glance at the greatcoats that still covered De Lancey's bed.

He gave them the latest news. Napoleon was still in Paris and was reported as trying to raise yet another army; the Duke had the Allied force on the march into France, and it was being strengthened daily with regiments sent out from England. Here, at Waterloo, his most pressing concern was to clean up the battlefield before the piles of dead should spread a pestilence through the area, and detachments were on their way to him from Wellington's army to assist.

After ten minutes, he made his excuses and departed about his business, but his visit had done both De Lanceys a world of good. It lifted their spirits to feel their presence here was now officially recognized; they had become part of the local establishment, so to speak. More importantly, they were assured of needed supplies; Magdalene had secretly grown worried about where they could find food to keep them from starving. Scovell had hardly been reassuring on this point, but at least they felt they would get whatever was available. And on leaving, he had told them that his surgeons, Powell and a newcomer named Woolricke, would call on them as often as their duties would permit, and he himself hoped to drop in from time to time to see how they were getting on.

Magdalene and her patient established a regular routine for the daily life of the cottage, with more or less set times for feeding and all the various ministrations required by a seriously injured man, and for the various chores of housekeeping. Emma, being a lady's maid, was no sort of cook and of little use around the cottage; Magdalene found it easier to look after most things herself, leaving Emma free, once she had swept out the cottage and washed the few breakfast dishes in the morning, to spend time in the village with the many friends she had managed to make among the wounded soldiers and orderlies there.

Left on their own for most of the time, with only one of the surgeons as an occasional visitor, the De Lanceys came to look on their tiny hovel as their home. William called it "our honeymoon cottage" and it became a game with them to pretend that they were planning improvements, or decorating it to suit their fancy.

"Uncle Oliver's picture would look well just there," De Lancey would say, gesturing to a blank wall. Uncle Oliver's picture was a private joke with them; a portrait of the celebrated cavalry officer, in an ornate gilt frame, it had been presented to William by his fellow officers when he had left his uncle's regiment as a young man, and it was virtually his only material possession.

On the morning of their third day together, Magdalene woke from a fitful sleep, or rather the series of catnaps which was all that she seemed able to manage, with a sense of foreboding. Sitting up beside her husband's bed, where De Lancey still slept, she became instantly aware of a strange smell. It seemed to be coming through the window, a frightful stink, infinitely revolting. Her gorge rose at it, and she held her nose as she got up and, going to the window, closed it as gently as she could. Tiptoeing back, she became aware that her husband had awakened and was staring silently at her.

"What a terrible smell!" she exclaimed. "Whatever can it be?"

"It's the smell of the battlefield," De Lancey responded. "The wind must have changed in the night, and is blowing in from the south."

Try as she might, Magdalene could not rid the room of that odious smell. Preparing breakfast—broth and bread was now the staple diet—amid such a stink of death seemed abhorrent to her, but she forced herself to arrange the morning meal in the usual way, and to persuade her patient to sip a few spoonfuls, although he waved away the bread, now grown stale and dry.

Later, as they sat conversing in low voices, because the smell seemed to have dampened their spirits and choked off their usual animated exchanges, they became aware of loud crackling sounds and the scent of smoke mingled with the battlefield smell. The noise grew louder and Magdalene, alarmed now and afraid that perhaps the dry grass and crops had somehow been set on fire, went out into the street to see what was the matter.

Towering columns of smoke were rising in the air, spreading as they rose and forming clouds of dirty gray that shut out the sun. The crackling noises grew still louder and Magdalene, now thoroughly alarmed, made her way down the street to the crest of the hill, where she looked out over the shallow valley below, a scene so frightful that she caught her breath.

The battlefield had been transformed into a vision of Hell. Smoke rose into the sky from a dozen enormous bonfires stoked by sweating soldiers, who appeared demon-like against the searing flames. Piled beside each fire were the bodies of horses, hundreds of them, and Magdalene could see parties of men adding still more bodies to the pyres. The smell of roasting flesh, strangely appetizing in a revolting way, was choking out the sickly stink of corruption, and the flames were quickly replaced by clouds of greasy black smoke as more carcasses were added.

But what made Magdalene gasp aloud were three tremendous pits, or, rather, trenches, ten feet wide and hundreds of feet long, dug deep into the floor of the valley.

Here the bodies of men, some stripped naked, others still clothed in uniform, were being flung helter-skelter into the depths. Magdalene could see that working parties, each equipped with several carts, were hard at work gathering up more bodies from where they had fallen, in every quarter of the field. British and French, infantry soldier or cavalry trooper, all alike now in the common anonymity of death, they were pitched into the carts like cordwood, and trundled off to the waiting pits. However heroic their end, whatever the agony of their last sacrifice, they were now just rotting flesh, and their bloated bodies, stripped of equipment and looted of anything of value, were tipped into the receiving earth. It was their numbers, as well as their terrible end, that appalled Magdalene; scores, hundreds, thousands of bodies were piled there.

Numbed with horror, unable to contemplate what she had seen, Magdalene turned away and made her way back up the mean street. It was a practical matter, she knew, the cleaning-up of a battlefield. She had heard Sir George Scovell discuss the procedure the previous day. Pestilence had to be avoided, weapons and equipment recovered; she had seen men tidily stacking usable arms and equipment in separate carts for reissue. But the loss of all individual character, the reduction of brave men to so much offal to be disposed of without ceremony in a garbage pit, shocked her beyond anything she had ever known. Wordless, pale, and miserable she made her way back to the cottage.

The street, the houses, everything about her seemed subtly changed. The lowering, smoke-darkened sky, the mean hovels, the peasants regarding her silently from half-opened doors, all seemed charged with evil. She had never before felt so alone, so frightened, in a dark, nightmare world, and she almost ran the last few steps that would take her back to her husband, and to their cottage, where she would find shelter and sanctuary.

Breathless, she burst through the door to find De Lancey smiling at her from his bed in the corner, and it was as though she was seeing him for the first time since the battle. She saw now how fragile he seemed; saw, for the first time, the sunken cheeks, the lines about the eyes and mouth, creases that pain had drawn on that dear face. He looked older and somehow shrunken, and she realized now, in a moment of terrible truth, that death was looking out at her from those smiling eyes. It was only a momentary glimpse, gone in a flash, but she knew now that he was dying, and that she must make the most of every precious moment together.

But he must never know; she must not show, by the least look or word, that she knew that he would never recover, and she smiled back at him as she came over and knelt at his bedside. The sickening battlefield smell would soon be gone, she assured him. Sir George Scovell had been as good as his word and the work of cleaning up the field was well under way. She could not describe in detail all the horrors she had seen, but De Lancey sensed somehow that she had been badly shaken and did not press for more, simply taking her hand in his and drawing her down, to rest her cheek against his.

That evening he seemed to be in an especially cheerful mood; in her heart, Magdalene now saw how, as his body grew weaker, his mood grew gentler and sweeter, and the knowledge made her almost dread his smile. He told her that he not only had become reconciled to his wound and the necessity it had brought him of becoming an invalid for a time, but now looked upon it as a blessing.

"There'll be no more wars for us, no more battles, no more separations," he told her. "My days as a soldier are over; we'll be able to live at peace now, just you and I, in Scotland." He went on to speculate on the sort of house they should get, and she forced herself to take an enthusiastic part in these fantasies, describing the features she would like to have in their new home, where she would like it to be, what she would like to grow in its garden, what color she should choose for the curtains to hang in its windows. It delighted her husband, she could see, to have such a project to mull over as he lay in the helpless immobility that gnawed at his self-respect. He obviously hated the frustrations and humiliations of being an invalid; of being fed, washed, and shaved, of enduring the indignities of the chamber pot, the leeches, and the endless probings and blood-lettings of the surgeons. To him, the prospect of their life together in some imaginary house in an imaginary place was all that kept him going, and Magdalene joined in the game with cheerful enthusiasm, even though she knew that it could never be.

In the days that followed, she flung herself into an all-out battle against the inevitable, striving to hold death at arm's length by sheer strength of will and body. She spent all her time at De Lancey's side, tending him, talking to him when he was awake, watching over him while he slept. She applied and removed the loathsome leeches as the surgeons insisted, she tore up her petticoat to make the compresses they recommended, she fed him the meals she prepared from their dwindling food supply.

Food had indeed become a pressing problem. Emma now got most of her meals by sharing with her soldier friends, but Magdalene was reduced to a turnip or two purchased from her peasant neighbors to eke out a precious loaf of bread. Whatever she had went to her patient; she herself ate hardly anything, since she could not bear to think that her husband's strength might fail because he was denied the food he needed. He was having increasing difficulty in breathing; sometimes he gasped for breath for long minutes at a time, while she held his hand and watched anxiously. Always after these paroxysms he would smile at her reassuringly, and she would resume her conversation as if the interruption had been of no consequence, but she could see that these spells were sapping his strength and causing him intense pain. Pain was something they both lived with, for they were as one now, bound together with such intensity that each sensed the other's feelings and was comforted by the depth of the other's love.

On the sixth day Magdalene grew seriously alarmed by De Lancey's rapidly worsening condition. He was now semi-conscious for periods of time, unable to sleep yet scarcely aware of what was going on about him. When she shaved him, as she did each day, he seemed to be staring at her without any sign of recognition. Most disturbing of all, he had developed a dry, rattling sound, deep in his chest, which constricted his breathing. Magdalene had heard of the death rattle experienced by dying men, and dreaded that this might be such a sound, and she was grateful that Woolricke chose this morning to call. He was a competent medical man in whose judgement she trusted, and he took particular interest in De Lancey, for whom he had a great admiration. He examined his patient closely, with his usual grave expression, which did not change when Magdalene stepped outside with him as he left. "Madam, I am afraid he cannot last much longer," he told her when she pressed him for an opinion. De Lancey's strength was ebbing fast; she must brace herself to face the inevitable and do what she could to make his last hours as easy as possible.

When she returned to the bedside she saw De Lancey's eyes on her. He smiled when she knelt at his side and began to reassure him, and after she had finished, rather lamely, he said simply: "I am dying, aren't I?"

She could not bring herself to answer. Her eyes filled with tears and without a word she took him gently in her arms and bowed her head over his, and for the first time in their short life together she gave herself up to grief, great sobs racking her body as she held him close. And it was now De Lancey's turn to soothe her, calming her until, suddenly ashamed of her weakness, Magdalene ceased her weeping and reasserted her normal, capable self.

For his part, De Lancey remained remarkably composed and serene. He was not afraid of dying, he told her; he had faced the imminent possibility of death many times before. But he could not bear to leave her, could not even bear the thought of ending their life together. It had been the happiest time he had ever known, short though it was, and these last shared days had brought them closer together than ever before. She was everything to him, he repeated, she had brought him happiness beyond anything he thought existed; nothing could compare in his life with the joy of her love. His composure broke; tears welled into his eyes, and it was now her turn to comfort and soothe him. She asked him if he believed in an afterlife. When he said he did, although he had no notion of what form it would take, she told him she was sure God would not part them for long, for He was a loving God and understood their need to share a common destiny.

That evening De Lancey would eat little except a few mouthfuls of broth, despite all Magdalene's urgings. She was alarmed at his inability to swallow more than the merest sips and grieved at his growing weakness, but she hid her feelings as best she could and passed the time talking to him of happy times they had shared together, the walks and rides and picnics of their courtship in Scotland. He listened with his eyes closed but with a smile on his lips as she relived those happy, carefree days before the shocking news of Napoleon's bid for power had set in train the march of events that had brought them both to Waterloo and this peasant's cottage.

The evening passed pleasantly enough and, after Emma had returned and gone to her cot upstairs in the loft,

Magdalene prepared her patient for bed, but De Lancey surprised her. "Darling," he whispered, "come into bed and sleep beside me, one last time."

She took off her dress with its long, full skirt and, gathering up the remains of her torn petticoat, she climbed carefully over him into the back of the narrow bed. There was just room for her between De Lancey, lying on his side, and the wall, and she snuggled down comfortably, with her arm around her husband's shoulder. They fell asleep quickly, being quite worn out, and slept the deep slumber of utter exhaustion, the first peaceful night-long sleep either had had all week in their tiny cottage.

Next morning, Magdalene was the first to waken. De Lancey was breathing with that dry, rattling noise again, which worried her, and, anxious not to wake him, she climbed slowly and carefully over him to the stone floor. She held a finger over her lips as Emma came down her ladder and the maid, with a nod to her mistress, passed silently out into the street, leaving them to their privacy. De Lancey awoke shortly afterward, his breathing shallow and spasmodic and obviously very weak. Once again, all he would swallow was a mouthful or two of broth, and he lay back then against the pillow, exhausted.

All morning Magdalene sat beside him with his hand in hers, talking in a low voice, De Lancey responding mostly with a gentle squeeze of her hand. Occasionally he would try to speak and she would bend her head to catch his whisper, and always he would tell her that she was all that mattered in his life, that she was his joy and his darling. And then his breath would fail him and he would fall silent, and she would kiss him and take up her low-voiced soothing, as his life gradually wound down.

The end came in the afternoon. The dry rattling noise increased and De Lancey struggled for breath. He was speechless now, his pulse weak and fluttering, and

Magdalene could feel his life ebbing away. She took him in her arms then, hot tears filling her eyes despite her efforts to hold them back. "Don't leave me, dearest, don't leave me!" she begged him, over and over. She felt a slight pressure on her hand, and then he was gone.

At twilight, when Emma returned to the cottage, she found her mistress still sitting on the bedside, silent in the darkness, with her dead husband's head on her breast.

12
Aftermath

MAGDALENE KEPT her composure, deliberately making her mind a blank, oblivious to all that had gone before. She had sent Emma to inform Sir George Scovell of De Lancey's death and had made the body presentable, straightening the bed and pulling a blanket up to obscure the face, before sitting down in a chair to await the coming of officialdom. Magdalene was very near the end of her tether but, by keeping a tight rein on her emotions, she was determined to carry through her duties properly.

In the event, however, officialdom proved too much for her. There was a peremptory knock on the door and in strode, not Sir George, but the odious Mr. Hume, as red-faced, brisk, and bluff as ever. "Well, young De Lancey's gone at last, has he?" he boomed, striding to the bed and throwing back the blanket.

It was too much for Magdalene. Bursting into tears, she mounted the ladder to the loft, where she threw herself full-length upon the cot and gave herself up to grief. Long after the indifferent Hume had carted the body off to his surgery, she lay there, racked by sobs, until a frightened Emma fetched Powell to attend her mistress. Sir George Scovell arrived, too, and at his insistence and with Emma's help, Magdalene was taken down and put to bed in the lower room. Worn out by endless nights without sleep, exhausted in mind and body by her exertions, and famished by a week virtually without food, she suffered a complete nervous collapse, and alarmed authorities sent to Britain to notify her family.

In the meantime an autopsy on De Lancey's body was carried out by Hume. It was found that eight ribs had been broken away from the spine by the fatal shot, and one of these had been badly smashed and driven through a lung. It was this puncture that was ultimately the cause of death, Hume announced, and the body was given up for burial.

Colonel Sir William Howe De Lancey, Knight Companion of the Bath and quartermaster general to the British Continental Army, was laid to rest in the cemetery of St. Jorge Ten Noode, a little Reformed Church on the Louvain road, a mile from Brussels, on the twenty-eighth of June, 1815, ten days after the battle in which he received his fatal wound. It was a simple ceremony, as his widow was unable to attend, and most of his friends and fellow officers were absent with the army in France. Sir George Scovell came with a few of his officers, and, as he had promised Magdalene, he had a simple headstone placed over the grave.

But if the ceremony itself was austere, the obituaries published in London were fulsome enough. Lieutenant-General Gore referred to De Lancey as "this incomparable officer," and Colonel Sir Augustus Fraser wrote, "De Lancey is our greatest loss; none can be greater, public or private."

Magdalene, after very nearly dying herself in the same bed where her husband had breathed his last, remained in very poor health. Much of the problem was mental; she repeatedly told her doctor that she had no wish to live, that her life had come to an end when De Lancey died in her arms. She made a visit to his grave early one morning when no one was about, and then her brother Basil arrived to take her home. He was shocked not only by her physical condition, but by her deep depression, and when they had returned to the family home at Dunglass, he set about the task of restoring her to her normal self.

All this grief, he pointed out, was a form of self-indulgence. He appealed to her deep religious beliefs. God had chosen, in His infinite wisdom, to take her husband from her. To repine so, to extend a normal grief for her loss indefinitely, was a sin, a questioning of God's will. In the end, her brother succeeded in returning Magdalene to something more like her usual self and a resigned acceptance of her fate, but she was never again the bright and gay young woman whose quick wit had so enchanted De Lancey.

As a dutiful daughter, she took up once again her role as chatelaine of her father's home. Persuaded that, as a young woman, she had a duty to marry and raise up children, in 1819 she married a Captain Henry Harvey of the Madras Light Infantry. An obscure middle-aged officer in a third-rate colonial regiment, totally without rank or ability, he was the complete antithesis of her brilliant first husband, and this may have been his principal recommendation. She proved a loyal and dutiful wife, and produced two children. Then, after three years of marriage to her now retired husband, she died on July 12, 1823, and went happily to her reward, for she had always believed she would be reunited with her De Lancey. She was just twenty-eight years old.

Today her tombstone, overgrown with lichen and quite forgotten, lies in the lovely little churchyard of St. Mary Magdalene and St. Peter, an ancient church nestled in a combe overlooking the Channel at Salcombe Regis in Devon.

As part of her convalescence after Waterloo, her brother had persuaded her, on her return to Dunglass, to set down on paper an account of her stay at Mont St. Jean. In 1905, nearly a century later, this was published in London as a booklet entitled *A Week at Waterloo in 1815,* edited by a Major B.R. Ward.

In 1889, to better commemorate the men who had fought and died in this, the world's most famous battle, an impressive new memorial was built near Waterloo. The bones of those who had been tossed into the huge pits after the action were exhumed and re-interred at the new memorial. At this time De Lancey's remains were moved from the now disused churchyard where they had been buried and placed, with those of a number of fellow officers, in the lovely cemetery of Evere, three miles northeast of Brussels.

The De Lancey reputation for distinguished service in time of war was perpetuated in later generations. A cousin of William's, Oliver De Lancey, became a famous officer of the Spanish Legion raised to fight against the Carlists in Spain, and died heroically at the head of his regiment in the defense of San Sebastian in 1837. A nephew of William's, E.W. De Lancey Lowe, became a major-general and won fame as the defender of the Lucknow residency during the Indian Mutiny of 1857.

The De Lancey legacy still survives in North America. The house on Broadway in New York City where William was born has long since disappeared and has been built over several times, but the ancestral De Lancey house, built by his grandfather, still stands in the city's financial district, at the corner of Broad and Pearl streets. The oldest building in New York City, it became a tavern run by a West Indian, Samuel Fraunces or Francis, and it is under that name that it survives today as a state-owned heritage building, with a fashionable restaurant on its ground floor. It was in its long room, once the De Lancey drawing room, that Washington bade farewell in 1788 to the officers of the Army of the Revolution.

De Lancey Street, on New York's lower East Side, is a reminder of William's uncle James, who owned property there in colonial times. Another uncle, Oliver, who, with his brigade, escorted a large group of Loyalists north from revolutionary New England into Canada to form the colony that later became the province of New Brunswick, is commemorated regularly with ceremony and pageantry in Fredericton, the provincial capital.

In Nova Scotia, King's-Edgehill School still lists De Lancey Barclay among its distinguished alumni, and in Toronto, Castle Frank perpetuates the name of De Lancey's brother officer, Francis Gwillim Simcoe, in the name given by his father, John Graves Simcoe, to the family cottage overlooking the Don Valley.

At Dunglass in Scotland, all that remains of Magdalene's lovely home is the little chapel, still the Collegiate Church of St. Mary, the impressive stables, now converted to a residence, and several small bridges. The old sundial and the hexagonal summerhouse, where William proposed to Magdalene, still stand on their grassy knoll, a reminder of happy times past.

But if the shades of the De Lanceys, those two star-crossed lovers, linger anywhere, it is at Waterloo. It is a curious fact that, although two great wars were to be waged over much of the ground of the 1815 campaign, and enormous battles involving millions of men and fought there over a period of years, Waterloo remains Belgium's best-remembered battlefield and one that is still visited each year by thousands of sightseers. The ridgetop site above the Allied center is today obscured by an enormous mound or pyramid of earth, heaped up as a memorial by the Belgians five years after the battle, and topped by a large stone lion. The elm tree above the Duke's command post at the crossroads, "Wellington's tree," as it came to be called, has long since disappeared, a victim to the insatiable hackings and sawings of souvenir hunters over the years.

The ridge is now covered with postcard booths and souvenir shops of every sort, but the battlefield itself is surprisingly unchanged from its 1815 appearance. The farmhouses of Mont St. Jean and Hougoumont are still there, little altered in appearance from the day when they were formidable fortresses, and ruined the bid of an Emperor to regain his throne. The little inn La Belle Alliance keeps alive its association with Ney and Napoleon, Blücher and Wellington, by selling postcards and labelled souvenirs, and is a favorite stop for bus tours. Enriched by the bodies of thousands of men and horses, the fields of the shallow valley and its gently sloping hillsides grow richer crops than the surrounding countryside, although the fields of rye that played such a part in the battle are no longer to be seen.

It is not difficult to understand the continuing appeal of Waterloo, and its hold upon the popular imagination. Unlike the battles of more modern wars, fought over huge areas for protracted periods of time, Waterloo was the last of Europe's decisive one-day battles, fought in a sort of cockpit that can easily be seen and understood by a viewer from a single vantage point. It featured a dramatic confrontation between a tyrannical Emperor, the greatest conqueror since Attila the Hun, and the gifted general appointed to defeat him. It was the last of the glamorous battles, fought by gorgeously uniformed armies at point-blank range, and often actually hand-to-hand. Its few instances of cowardice and desertion merely emphasized the outpouring of bravery on both sides, the gallantry of the cavalry and the grim endurance of the infantry. It also introduced new elements in the waging of war: the sustained cannonading, the greatest ever known to that time, presaging the still greater role of artillery in the wars to come. And it marked the climactic moment in that most spectacular of battlefield operations, the cavalry charge. Never again would the world witness such a tremendous onfall of massed cavalry as that which shook the ground at Waterloo.

Yet along with all the glitter and the glory, it is the sheer brutality and hardship of the battle and its aftermath that most impress the modern visitor: the endurance of discomfort and pain, the inadequacy of the commissariat, and the casual butchery of the surgery. It was a hard, brutal age, seeming infinitely remote from our modern, effete era, yet so surprisingly close in time; many of our great-grandfathers and even a few of our grandfathers knew men who fought at Waterloo.

Some of the tourists who visit the place today seem more concerned with fiction than with fact, for Waterloo is a battlefield burdened with a hundred myths. There is the fiction of the famous "sunken road" into which an unsuspecting French cavalry regiment is supposed to have ridden with calamitous results. But for that road, so the story goes, Wellington's army would have been overwhelmed. There is the equally popular myth concerning General Cambronne, commanding Napoleon's famed Old Guard, who is supposed to have said, in reply to a summons to surrender in the dying moments of the battle, "The Old Guard dies, the Old Guard does not surrender." (In fact, Cambronne took good care to surrender himself the moment things took a turn for the worse, and survived happily, however ungallantly, into a ripe old age. His more likely, if ruder, retort was simply: "*Merde!*")

As for the Old Guard, that most élite of all élite corps, it is surely a monstrous irony that this unit, victorious in a hundred encounters, should be best remembered in popular history for its single dramatic and decisive defeat. "*La Garde recule!*" is one of the great despairing cries of all time.

There is no trace today in Mont St. Jean of the little peasant's hovel that was the De Lanceys' "honeymoon cottage." In all likelihood it was pulled down and replaced by one of the cottages that line the single street of the little hamlet today. It was a ramshackle building, already old when the De Lanceys knew it, and there was no reason for its Belgian owner to preserve it. The street is much busier today than it was then, but few of the visitors who throng it are aware of the drama played out there so long ago.

In the evening, though, when the last tourist bus has departed and the souvenir shops have closed for the night, the battlefield beyond the buildings comes into its own. As the light fades and the dusk draws in, it is easy to picture those shadowed slopes covered with heaps of men and horses, the bodies of the dead and dying, just as they must have been on that dreadful June night. In the evening, Waterloo is a spectral place, haunted by the ghosts of the soldiers who died on this field. Here, countless thousands of life stories were cut short, the dramas being lived by all those husbands, lovers, and sons. Their stories must remain forever untold, forever unheard, for all the ghostly keening the imagination detects on the evening breeze from the darkening battlefield. This love story of a brave soldier and his devoted young bride, which ended so tragically on the edge of this valley, must speak for all.